The Lake

by William Schubert

BETTER BRAINS BOOKS

The Lakefront

William Schumpert

Published by Better Brains Books, 2021.

This is a work of fiction. Similarities to real people, places, or events are entirely coincidental.

THE LAKEFRONT

First edition. February 25, 2021.

Copyright © 2021 William Schumpert.

ISBN: 979-8201229900

Written by William Schumpert.

Table of Contents

Title Page 1

River Falls 6

Reign 13

Silence 20

And They Call Her Siri 27

First Strike 34

Eye of the Storm 41

Seven 48

Happy Times Again 55

Bread 62

Déjà Vu 69

All's Well That Ends Well 76

Dance of the Cherubs 81

Claro De Luna 86

River Falls

Blue skies and clouds riding on the gentle breeze is all I can see now. Driving down this old highway brings back so many memories for me. Knowing that I'll be returning to my hometown of River Falls. It brings a sigh of relief to my weary self, always working for the big wigs in the big city life. Not that I have anything against the city that I work in- no. It can't beat those hot summers that we shared, down by the lake and sipping ice cold lemonade. Mom could make that so perfect. We were living it on cloud nine with the July sun floating in the milky blue. Not a cloud to bother its happiness; and the winter was even better. Then came the cool breeze of the fall and its gentle embrace of the sweet country fairs. And we would bundle in all the coats and blankets. Mom would once again work magic. Those delicious hot chocolate drinks and gingerbread houses.

"What would you like for Christmas? I know you've been a very good boy this year and you deserve all the wishes your hearts desire."

A Santa at a mall outlet could never bring the warm love that a mother or father could give a child. All those heart filled memories and gently placed pictures in my mind. You can never escape the past, no matter how good or bad it may have been. It's always a part of you. These distant, wonderful memories can often times hit you when you least expect it. I almost forgot about them so fast being so occupied by work. The forced negativity of pushing papers around and meeting the deadline. You have your due dates for the proposal. Don't forget the scheduled for meetings with those blood sucking bureaucrats and landowners. That kind of pressure tied me in. So much I nearly forgot that unforgettable summer when I turned eight. The worst birthday of my life but it turned out to be one of the best. Mom asked me where I wanted to spend my birthday. And as she asked I already knew my favorite place was down by the lakefront. The lake was a special place in my heart. The hideout I would always go to only for special occasions with special friends. Even by myself when I felt like crying my troubles away. It was there I met my friend Ben- old round faced Ben was a real 'knuckle-head' as we called him. He was the goofiest and yet most earnest and strict kid I ever knew. It was way back when I first moved to River Falls. I decided to do some exploration of the area and what did I find? The biggest and the most luxurious body of water I have ever laid eyes on. It was no mere body of water but rather a luxurious mirrored image of the sky lying in the middle of the woods. It was so crisp and beautiful as the sun sparkled in its glory as if the lake itself helped to warm the sun. As I conjured with this heavenly presence a big pudgy kid came tumbling in from the woods. I was guessing that he was trying not to be seen by anyone but let's admit it. Ben could stick out like a sore thumb in any situation from any angle at any given time. As I smiled at this situation I was about to burst out into laughter. That is until I noticed that the kid had tears coming down his cheeks. He then began to hustle down to the water as he noticed me. It was an awkward moment. We both stood there staring at each other. Neither of us expected any company to show up. We were both in a state of shock realizing that someone else seemed to show up out of the blue. And there we were staring at each other. And for what seemed to be an eternity. Gazing into each others souls trying to see who the other was and why that other was there. And it was after that long and deranged moment of silence that Ben turned the other way. He snuffled his nose and wiping his face, trying to look tough.

"So what, you've never seen a fat kid before?" Was all that came from him as he continued to wipe his face.

"Well I have".

He turned to me with an angry look in his eyes. The size of this kid! But luckily for me his angry face transformed into that of happiness. He began chuckling at my odd comment.

"How big?"

"I've seen way bigger kids. This one fat kid I used to know at my old school. He always carried around Twinkies in his bag and they got squished between all his books. Anytime we ran into him we told him to stop killing our snack food."

At this comment Ben bellowed out the happiest, the most humble laugh I have ever heard in my life. The kind of laugh that was waiting inside when you feel upset or lonely. And from the sound of his laughter Ben must have been alone for a long time. It's unfortunate because Ben was a kindhearted guy. He was smart for someone his age and always knew a lot of good jokes. Perhaps it was more by destiny than just chance that we found each other that day by the lake. It was hard for me to move away from what I had called home for such a long time. Moving can be tough for a child after making best friends that you thought you'd spend your entire life with. Then only to realize that you have to say goodbye to them forever. I guess it was tough for Ben to be with anybody, to let alone even have a best friend to be with.

"You should write to Twinkie's mom. Tell her that her kids are being killed by a fad kid" came out of the laughing mouth of Ben.

"Yeah and hold that kid for ransom!"

After my response it seemed like we laughed for over ten minutes that warm summer day. As if we couldn't help our selves. We laughed and laughed, and laughed so much I thought I was going to die from laughing. And finally after all that laughing we decided to get up. We collected some stones by the water and threw a dozen or two. The ripples on the last seemed to echo forever out into the vast emptiness. What appeared to be a majestic image of the endless heavens. A mirror into a whole other world tapped by the consistency of a ripple in its continuum. The site of it dazzled my senses and I could see Ben was struck in awe as well as he gazed dumbfounded at the site. It was at this moment of revelation we were free from its magnificent charm. And we began to slowly but surly speak to one another. Ben was the first to speak-

"So you're new around here?"

"Yeah- how do did you know?"

"Only a new kid wouldn't have known about me-"

"You mean about being-"

As out spoken Ben was he was also very shy and timid. The poor kid started to turn the other way with tears in his eyes.

"So what?"

"I don't care. Who cares if you're fat? I don't!"

"You don't?"

"Don't see why not. You seem like a neat guy."

"Yeah well... not everyone seems to think so."

"Who's everyone? I haven't met them yet"

Not the most logical reasoning but it got to Ben as he gave another hearty chuckle.

""Everyone" isn't a name- you seem like a goofy kid!"

"I don't care about that either! It only matters what I think about myself!"

And with a deep sigh of relief Ben responded, "If only I could feel like that-".

"What, feel good about yourself?"

"Yeah..."

"Well you feel good right now don't you?"

"Yeah I do-"

"No one made me laugh for as long as you did, and to me you seem like a neat guy. Who cares what everyone else thinks. How about you and me think about what we think?"

Ben was known to slouch when sitting. But it was at that moment I saw him actually sit up straight, as if a revelation occurred in his mind. His eyes seemed to twinkle as a huge smile began to fill his face.

"That actually ain't bad of an idea- in fact I like it! From now on I'm only going to care about what I think and what my new best pal thinks. By the way my name is Ben- what's yours?"

What's yours?

What's yours?

What's yours?

Sorry... I must have been rambling on about my past and got stuck somewhere. The birthday party- I arranged it with Mom about a year after I met Ben. It was a warm and sunny summer at that. The hottest I can remember. And on a hot day in June when my friends were all at camp or stuck with their relatives for the summer. For my eighth birthday I wanted it to be with my Mom. And if you're wondering what happened to Dad... Well he died in a boating accident around the time I was born. Beyond that I didn't know very much about him and I guess Mom never told me to ensure that I wouldn't be hurt. Well Father or no Father I still wanted my favorite person in the world to be with me at my big birthday. To me the number eight was mine and mine alone. It seemed to be a lucky charm. The first word I ever said (at least that's what Mom keeps telling me) and it stuck with me ever since then. Perhaps the number itself never brought me luck. But it still had an important meaning, and my eighth birthday had to be that important. Come again I guess the number didn't bring me any luck. Turns out we had to drag along my little four year old sister Cindy to the birthday party as well. You know the 'monkey see monkey do' syndrome? Well Cindy was born with it and she intended to articulate it with me everyday at every moment. It may have seemed like a drag but a deal was a deal. And if I wanted to have the best birthday party at the lake some sacrifices had to be made.

The day finally came. We had Mom's delicious home made grilled cheese sandwiches for lunch. The kind that would melt so smooth in your mouth. And all while drinking iced lemonade that soothed the summer's heat. After this favorite dish we grabbed the wrapped presents and started out to the lake near our house. I could tell that this was going to be the best birthday ever.

I don't remember very much of it beyond the fact that I kept on saying it was the best of my life. There was the moment when we finally arrived at the lake. Cindy went from being the girl who always copied your movement to the whiny runt who never got her way. The party you had to attend knowing you had to help. But you never got the presents or gratitude for helping; must have been a stage in life I guess. The stage that kicked in proceeded by the constant whines of "Mommy when do I get to open a present?" and "I don't want to go anymore!" Mom was of course the negotiator in our constant fusses as she offered her kindness to calm our menacing

"Now honey your birthday is in a few months, you can have a birthday present when it's your birthday."

"But I want one now!"

"Well you'll have to wait your turn. Your birthday present will be especially for you and no one else."

"For me?"

"That's right Cindy- a special present made for you. But you'll have to be a good girl and be patient until that time."

"Did you hear that? My present's going to be special. You can have your own stupid presents."

To this logic I only rolled my eyes in disbelief. How gullible she seemed to be, but whatever it took to keep her quiet was fine with me. Cindy's newly found confidence inspired her to be more enthusiastic. She even carried most of the presents, only leaving Mom with about one or two in the back.

It was after this that things seem to become vague in detail. We were all sitting on the dock eating sandwiches starring into the blue sky... What a beautiful blue sky it was. So warm and magnificent in its solitude. There was the blue sky and... if only I could have remembered what it was Mom said to me at that moment. Her gorgeous lips moved in a heavenly symphony. The words flew from her gentle thoughts, but it's hard to remember what she said. Then I'm getting ready to jump into the lake, ready for my first swim of the summer. I ran, and I ran for what seemed to be forever. It was as if everything were slowing down right in front of me, as if time took a moment to pause. As I ran and as I came closer to the river I told myself to jump but I didn't heed to what sounded like yelling. Into the lake head first, and for what seemed to be for an eternity...

Damn eighteen-wheelers! I swear that he would have been a few feet closer to my car I would have been crushed! Forgot how unforgiving these roads can be and how poorly the people can drive. It's especially hard since it's beginning to rain. I had to be the lucky man out and about on the road at that time. Well the rain isn't that bad. This jackass of a driver in front of me is making it hard to steer this narrow roadway. And as if it couldn't get any better the driver was swerving left and right in a very lazy way. First he barley passes me. Now he ignores the rules of driving! The driver must have been deaf or hard of hearing as I honked my horn. But no effect on his sad interpretation of steering a massive vehicle.

'River Falls- 3 Miles' read the sign.

Finally the detour was coming up. I don't think I could have lasted much longer with this guy in front of me. Pure music to my ears as I knew that I was only miles away from my old home town. From my friends and family that I haven't seen in such a long time. And for what seems like years after being so cooped up with work.

The rain seems to be starting up; it's getting harder to see the road. I better take this detour slowly...

Reign

The storm seems to be getting harder. Hate it when the weatherman says that it's going to be a cloudless, blue day of sunshine. Then he's hit by the contradiction that nature does whatever she desires. Well whoever's to blame for all this- nature or the mislead news it still makes it difficult. Knowing this stubborn jackass of a driver won't stop with his lack of driving skills. Three miles may not seem that far for the average driver out on the freeway. But behind this kind of situation a minute doubles into tenfold. The exit- that sweet and delightful glee of utter salvation.

'River Falls- 2 Miles'

Only two more miles to go as I pass the exit to some recreational park. Funny it felt like two more miles two miles ago. Life has its funny ways of catching up to you when you least expect it.

"River Falls- 1 Mile"

One mile was even more of a breath of fresh air to this tiresome traveler. One mile to go; only one more before I'm finally able to-

'River Falls- ½ Mile'

One half mile to go; since when did a half mile become an accurate measurement for travel? And the eighteen-wheeler never ceases to swerve left and right...

'River Falls- ¼ Mile'

One fourth mile. Now that tops the cake of utter nonsense. A one fourth of a measurement that in itself makes no sense to announce to the world. I'm not too sure but Alice in Wonderland was a take on the ridiculous usage of modern age math. And if it is then I hurled myself into the rabbit hole in search of my dear Dinah.

'River Falls- Next Right'

At last! Things are starting to look up as I turned on my turning signal. So eager to finally drive on the road that took what seemed like a lifetime to find. And as I was turning the rain continued to pour down, beating my car like golf balls hitting the green. The windshield wipers seemed to sweat from the exhausting labor of panting up and down the glass. And as the windshields beat heavily I found myself sweating to the heavy air that burst from the car's defog. It seemed to have little to no affect on the ever increasing power of nature and her fury. Go into the turn nice and smooth I said to myself... Nice and smooth now... Not too fast! Not too fast now... Finally that turn was a success after making my way from the road to the exit. As uneasy as I felt going down that eerie detour blackened by rain I felt the soothing relief. Not only was the eighteen-wheeler not in front of me but that I was that much closer to River Falls. The relief that I was soon going to see my old home town for the first time. And what would seem like decades. It gave me the courage and strength to continue through the storm that lay ahead of me. After all on the other side of chaos is peace. But for now the chaos seems to be without end as I go slower and slower down this old road. It would be nice if I could remember driving down it in the past. But my mind only draws blank. My entire surrounding is covered with nothing but falling water. The ocean itself? The only thing I can concentrate on is the perking roadway. It tips left and right as if to tease my senses in a time of utter madness. I check the speedometer and I'm only going about five miles. But it's as if I'm going ninety miles an hour on a thirty mile road. I'm gripping the wheel with every bit of my strength hoping that what I'm driving on is the road. Yet it seemed that the slower I went the faster it seemed; the more cautious I was the more dangerous it was feeling. But careful not to let my mind play tricks on me. I continued to go slow and cautious, no matter what the consequences would bring. Well the road was still in front of me and I was still on the right side of it, or at least what was believed to be the right side. No bumps from driving so I haven't hit anything. So far it seems to be so good- I hoped it would stay that way.

And as I was making my way in this mother of all storms I swore that I saw something. What appeared to be a small shadow glaring to the side of the road. It was one of the most captivating scenes that I could recall. It appeared to be a short. A dark outline and yet it stood there so long and elongated, a dreamlike sequence within a nightmare. And those beady white-eyes... God I could not recall such horrifying eyes. But were they eyes? Could they in fact have been fire glaring into my very soul? The very presence of these illuminated "things"... It struck my very heart, my very inner being with terror as I kept telling myself to slow down. I have to keep on the road I kept reminding myself as I remembered the storm that surrounded me. I need to slow down. God I need to slow down.

I listened to the utter cries from within my inner conscience as I forced my foot to lean heavier on the brake. But that shadow- that foreboding presence... As hard as I tried I could not ignore its presence. It was haunting me more and more as I fought to withhold my very sanity, and it was at last I could bear no more of it. I knew that if I didn't pull over then I would go insane. Knowing this I pushed on the brakes as hard as I ever pushed and slowly detoured to the side. Assuring that my car's position would not force any coming drivers to meet the same fate as I, or worse. I turned the wheel and the car caressed to the side. It seemed that everything was slowing down... Trying to calm itself by stopping time's everlasting flow. I had no doubt in my mind that at that moment time was never a consistent cycle. But rather a cycle with what appeared to be many tracks. for it was that moment I felt that I hit one of those many tracks as I made my way to the side of the road. On my way there the thought of that haunting creature that lurked not so long ago-

It tortured by inner being. And yet as hard as I looked outside I could not find its foreboding presence where it once stood. For it was not that monstrous creature luring in front of my car. But rather the shadow of what appeared to be a small child. It was the silhouette of pure and tendered innocence. At this realization time gave to after grinding to a halt. The breaks squealing as the car breached the curve.

The car's front lights portrayed what was indeed a small child standing out in the hard, cold rain. standing there in the middle of what appeared to be a storm of apocalyptic proportions. From his beckoning I then began to regain sense as the car finally came to a halt. As I prepared to open the door I couldn't help but notice that the child was just standing there. It was both tragic and horrifying. My heart raced as I felt bestowed to rescue a child in aid. Yet the haunting glare of his lifeless appearance... It drew me away from the pride of selflessness. With heart still beating and hairs standing on end I thrust the door open. And I entered the forbidding madness. The rain beat as I fought with all my might to reach that poor child- and still he stood there. Was he afraid of the rain, afraid of me? Well for whatever the reason I didn't dwell on it. As I came closer I was able to finally see the child. A small boy, no older than four or five, wearing a buttoned up white shirt and khaki shorts. His short hair wavered in the rain, as he was drenched from head to toe, looking as if he were crying. I gestured the boy to enter the car as I could hear nothing in the cataclysmic storm. And the boy immediately dashed for the driver's side of the vehicle. He stood waiting for me to enter the car. And when I did he threw the door open in anticipation and upon entering he closed it with all his might.

At first he sat there as if he were collecting himself from an agonizing ordeal, and who could blame him? The poor kid was overflowing with water, drenched from head to toe as he shivered from toe to head. It was a moment later he was finally able to cease from the twitching.

"Thanks for the help".

"It's not a problem- what's your name?" I replied as calm as a man could be to a child in need.

"Oh my name- my name is-" he began to stutter out as he gave a loud sneeze. He wiped his nose with his wet sleeve as I reached for an available handkerchief. He accepted it as he blew into it and jabbed the handkerchief into his still soggy shorts. I decided to leave out some extra in case as I prepared to start driving once again. This time remembering that I needed to be even more cautious now that a child was riding with me.

"So where are you headed?" I asked as I made my way back to the road.

"Well- the problem mister is- well it's- it's that…"

"What is it?"

I couldn't see him as I was paying full attention on the road. The rain commenced even further but his reflection looked as if he were beginning to somber. "I- I tried to run away from home and I don't know how to get back…"

Now he began the old "boo hoo" routine you would expect from someone his age. Yet it was a very sad cry that made one feel guilty or neglectful. I couldn't pat him on the shoulder, as my hands were concentrated on the road so I did my best to calm the poor boy down.

"Hey it's all right. Where are you from? I can drive you to your town and we'll be able to find out where your parents are."

I was glad to hear his voice to be more settle and calm as he responded- "It's a place called River Falls. It's not that far from here mister."

"I know where that is! I used to live there and I'm on my way there to meet with my family." He gave no response but I could imagine he was feeling much better now. "We'll stop by a local office and they should be able to help you out from there. How does that sound?"

"Thanks mister- um mister-"

"Matt. My name is Matt."

"Well- thank you Mr. Matt sir."

To his innocent comment I couldn't help but give a light chuckle. "Well you're very welcome."

I made my way from the curve back onto what I could best assume to be the road. I was more concentrated than ever to reach River Falls for the safety of the boy. And as glad as I was to aid those in need there was an intense sting from the cold rain that chilled my bones...

It brings back the memories of that Christmas following that special birthday. There was snow everywhere, and it was so cold- the coldest winter I can remember. Even the lake that I adored all my life. The one that shined with so much love and aspiration. Left to nothing more than an icy prison, the stronghold of all that ray of life locked away. The path that we made to the lake was long lost under the massive snow and ice. Never to be found until its enchanted spell would done away by a miracle. And those were hard to come by in such a frigid atmosphere. The old rubber tire swing that hung underneath the tree by the cozy cottage. Buried by the vast darkness of winter as the ice devoured its outer cover. And the house. It seemed colder than the snow that covered it. A bitter chill that reflected from what windows that were not submerged by the old winter's touch. The door looked to be frigid, and its handle was a ball of thick decayed ice. One touch would make the hands numb and send the chills running through the spine. And in this thick layer of cold death I saw my mother and little Cindy. They cuddled by the fire sipping on hot chocolate. All wrapped up in layers and layers of blankets as I stood near the Christmas tree looking for presents. I didn't find any and I became upset. I made a tantrum of how devastated I was for not finding one present with Christmas so close. But they ignored me as they always did when I threw fits in such immature matters. Still I commenced in my contestant stomping around the tree in protest. And yet the harder I stomped the more they ignored my utter cry of pity. And my constant echo of woes were only heard by the darkness. And it was then that it hit me...

It hit me!

It hit me!

For God's sake right ahead of me lay a railing twisting towards the opposite direction. And as hard as I tried I could not for the likes of me steer the wheel away from it. I saw that turn ahead of the pouring rain and as the rain poured on my window with ever fiber of my body. Every bit of energy, blood and sweat to steer the car away from catastrophe. And as time itself began shifting slower the car began to slip out of control. There was a large echoing bang from the wreckage. I quickly turned towards the boy to assure his safety.

"Hey kid are-"

But he wasn't there!

Silence

How could a child disappear like that? The storm was still as furious as ever and... the rain... it seemed to have stopped; it was gone, along with the kid it vanished into thin air. And as the fog and the raindrops ceased to be I finally had a good look at the mess I made. It turns out the car hit the curve of a sharp turn pretty bad- so bad that my car wouldn't start. The only noise it made as I turned the keys in the ignition was a squealing hiss of pain. It followed with the dying putter of the engine. It was not much of a surprise for me. But the frustration and anger came from two facts. The first being the safety of the child. The other is I had no idea where I was. Or at least I didn't recognize it very well due to all the fog across the road and the sky.

Sitting in the car wasn't going to fix anything (or the car for that matter). I decided to get out and try to figure out where exactly I was. After stepping out of the car I walked a few paces forward. Amidst all this fog I felt that I was stumbling through a dark room but the darkness was grey and white. A light wind picked up a good chunk of it and I saw a sign that brought relief to my weary soul- "Welcome to River Falls".

I must have entered from the West road. The one Mom rarely took because she thought the sign was too big for such a nice small town. It doesn't look like time has been on its side either. Judging from its grotesque and abnormal appearance. Empty spider webs hanging all over as the rotting wood smelled like a burning acid. As the carved name twisted and charred over the years of decay. I was surprised to not see a detour or end of road sign barricading this God forsaken sight.

But whatever the reason for this monstrosity I finally made it. And it's more than likely the kid somehow made his way into town- a little scared from a stranger.

Sick to my stomach from the stench and the awful sight I moved forward. Fortunately I felt a light breeze messaging my arm. I was beginning to see what appeared to be a twisted roadway that arched to the South as Vincent Hill lay behind it. Even though I still couldn't see too well due to the fog. I knew that Vincent Hill lay ahead. Mom never took the South exit from town but she always adored the hillside. And often times spoke about how one day having a hike down a trail. But of course there was something that always kept her away from entering this South roadway. And to this day I still have no idea what it is (note to self: ask Mom about Vincent Hill). The fog was dying out as I continued on my way to River Falls. The picture ahead of me was getting clearer now. A sharp arch as I thought, and behind it was sure enough Vincent Hill. It had that distinguished characteristic that set it apart from other parts of town. That special monument of a structure that wasn't afraid to stick out like a sore thumb. And as sore of a thumb Vincent Hill was it made its reputation of being a beauty mark. A gorgeous display of wildlife and trees as far as the eye could see. Surrounded by the lazy clouds and milky blue sky. And when the rain came in Vincent Hill continued its parade with no hesitation. It looked even more magnificent when drenched by all the water. If only I could see it now- still too much fog covering it. And as that came into thought. I stopped for a moment to ponder whether the kid might have retreated into the hillside. Should I continue on the road or make my way near the base of Vincent Hill? But that would seem too risky of a move, even for a kid. Besides he said he was from River Falls and the fog is beginning to clear up. So with that brief thought I made my way down the road. I picked up my pace as I saw the fog was starting to wisp away.

Passing the arch the road became straight as it leads forward. I looked back and could see Vincent Hill much clearer now. Even with all the fog still climbing atop its side- it's such an elegant display and quite a sight for my weary eyes. In fact when I get to Mom's house I'm not only going to ask her about Vincent Hill. I'm going to propose- no insist that we take a hike up Vincent Hill. A good hike in the woods would do the both of us good for our health and we'd be able to catch up on lost times. But until then I have to find that kid... No I haven't forgotten about him at all. turning around so much wouldn't be such a good idea. Especially since the fog is building up around me in an unusual matter. It seems to be collecting itself all around, as if it were in command of its own movement and acted on self judgment. But what that judgment could be I don't know. All I did know that this point was that River Falls somehow lied ahead of me. And somewhere in this utter darkness of fog a little kid might be lost in search of his family. But is the fog preventing me from finding River Falls, or the boy, and if so then why? But such a ridiculous notion- how could a natural cause like wind and fog have a mind of its own? I'm just thinking too much, or too little on what I should be doing rather than what could happen. So casting away any utter nonsense I commenced forward into the gentle waltz of the fog. Observing its peculiar movement and paces I swept my arm left and right to make a clear view of what was ahead of me. It would seem ironic to describe the fog's movement as a waltz. After all the circumstances that have occurred but there was no other way to explain it. It was both enchanting and haunting the way it lapsed around me. Giving that outrageous notion that nature itself was acting on its own free will. the most horrifying thing about it is... is it acting on its own? To this thought I paused for a moment. And the hair on the back of my neck paused as well. It stood on end as the memory of those ghastly eyes from the road way came to memory. But why now?

Oh my God...

Those eyes- the red eyes that starred into my very soul back on the road- they were in the fog! Right before me I saw what appeared to be gleaming rays of blood red starring at me. Two small red lights peering right at me. And thank God that the fog covered the surrounding for what horrors lay ahead of me I dare not see. At the first sight my knees began to tremble as my heart raced and goose bumps developed all over my shaking body. It was the first time in a very long time that I felt the coldness of fear in my heart. The very things of nightmares and misery was standing before me as I trembled like a lost child...

But the child- there's a kid out there who needs help. I stood there in fright of what may lie ahead of me. Soon I realized that he could be in a much worse circumstance. And with that thought I gestured my arm forward to wisp away the darkness. I became more intense and more scarred. But I kept hurling my arm forward knowing that I was going to hit something very soon. And I continued to swing as hard as I could and as fast I could swing. My arm grew tired and my goose bumps died out to give birth to the sweat that encompassed my skin. My heart beat faster and I felt sure something had to give before I would succumb to the madness around me. There had to be an end to it! For God's sake there must be an end to this menacing chaos!

And then it hit me- it hit me this time, or rather I hit it. As the fog breezed away from my constant rage of violent swiping I saw that I banged my arm- on a stop sign. A stop sign that was on the corner of a street! A building lay there on that corner behind the stop sign. And as the fear built within me it left just as fast as I began to see that I was finally home in River Falls! The fog was departing and as it did I saw my surroundings much clearer. The stop sign that I hit laid on the corner of Landers Street, right next to the old First National Bank Mom always used. It was all coming back to me now! The fog retreated once more. The other side of the street showcased the old buildings of the downtown district. most seemed to be abandoned and shackled as I remembered them. It was then I had to pause for a moment and take a breath. It was due to the throbbing pain in my arm, but the flooding of memories served as the perfect remedy for my pain. The fog resided outside of town but was still very strong with only a few lying around the concrete and the road. The sight was so much clearer now. It's hard to believe that a storm was brewing a little while ago. It seemed to equal that of biblical proportions and now it looks as if a gentle storm made its way by. Not only was that a peculiar thought but what was even more baffling was that no one was out and around. Where is everyone? The question rang in my head as I peered left and right. Yes the bank was right there and the old downtown buildings across the street. The bakery and the market were a few miles south in the more robust part of the downtown area. But even for this "slump" I expected to at least see a few people out and about during the day. After all it was a Tuesday and the bank had to be open, and it's the only bank in town for as long as I could remember.

At first I thought there may have been some festival or carnival going on. The townsfolk always loved the carnivals that came to town in those golden-leafed autumn times... But the only problem is that it was the middle of August and no festivals that I knew of took place around this time. A special festival was about to take place? I even kid with the foolish notion that the entire town was planning a surprise party in my honor. How childish I am to imagine an event, and the idea made me blush.

But what's this? My attention shifted towards the alley way as I swore that I saw what appeared to be a long shadow. But shadows that long- how could a shadow be casted so long down an alley? The size of it seemed to encompass the entire alley and part of the street. A size so devastating I could not imagine how large the person casting it may have been- but could it be... inhuman? I knew deep down I didn't want to find out. But somehow I took the courage to follow this shadow, and I crept ever so to the corner of the alley way. As I looked into the darkness I saw the phantom once again. An elongated shadow-shaped like a person hunching forward. It moved and I followed its traces into the silent echoes. My knees shook in madness and I began to sweat all over. I couldn't bear the horror of seeing who was casting such a ghastly shadow and I retreated back to the street. What was to be a welcoming sight soon turned to confusion as I saw other shadows casted on the buildings. The bank displayed a frightful sight as a larger shadow crept its way along the wall. And yet it vanished into thin air. I looked once again only to find the shadow was gone- but there it was once more! This time it lay on the old abounded warehouse across the street. It to disappeared as I saw the figure on another nearby building. I kept following its movement but its dance of terror seemed to begin all around me. It found its way from the bank all the way to the old furniture store. Only to return to the other side of the street and back to the bank. As if it were running in circles around me but rather it was lurking. The figure hunched and made its way from one building to the other. Around the corner and back again it went as if it were playing a deadly game of cat and mouse. By the second lap I had begun to crouch in fear of what was happening around me. If it were playing a game what was its intention? What role would I play in this insane spectacle? Already my heart was pounding. And the fear had grown larger than the figure that haunted me. The constant lurking of the shadow began to crush my sanity.

I cried out for help and spouted curses at that damned figure. I sat there in the street helpless from the chaos encircling me. Like the storm it seemed to have a power of its own, an ungodly appearance that shook my very soul and every bone in my body. But unlike the storm I could find neither remorse nor courage to carry forward. It was at that moment I felt the very piercing of my innocence. Devoured by the cold blackness of horror as the shadow danced around me. And in glee towards my shallower state. And it was at that dark hour that I saw it once again... the dark red eyes emerged from the shadow. The eyes that followed me into River Falls were starring into me once more- it was a living nightmare in the flesh. God help me I thought to myself. God help me...

How long is this going to last? How long did this Hell on Earth intend to haunt my soul? Why is it happening and why is it happening to me? The questions raced through my mind as I sat there frozen in fear. I kept asking myself How long is this going to last? I beg you God I beg you!

It would seem the demons casted out as I felt a sharp sting of pain on my back. The hit lunged me to the ground. And that was the last I saw of that ghastly shadow and its peering eyes of red sin as I began to fade out of consciousness...

And They Call Her Siri

I was never hit as hard as I was at that moment. That piercing sensation that lasted for a few seconds...

The only thing that came to mind was that stinging in my back. I felt conflicted by such a massive throb as I lay there... but where I didn't know. At this point I didn't even think to open my eyes, in fear of the gruesome result of the aftermath. What if I were in a hospital bed paralyzed from the waist down? I don't think I could take that kind of reality even if it were mine. And I didn't want to wake up to such an unbearable nightmare that I could never escape. So I decided to lie there. What felt like a comfortable establishment. Like a sofa of some kind but it didn't feel like a bed, or a hospital bed for that matter. This realization brought comfort to my doubtful self. It was such a relief knowing that I wasn't trapped in such a situation as I had assumed. To make things better I could feel my toes wiggling on the ends of my feet. anticipated to move on the ground once more. My fingers began to flutter as well and I slowly but surly opened my weary eyes.

And what I woke up to was no horror story- it was in fact a wooden ceiling as I noticed that I was on a black leather couch. I was very concerned and alert towards the unknown surrounding but I found that I couldn't get up. I wasn't tied down to anything but rather my body was bound by weakness. I found myself helpless on that sofa. The only thing I could move were my head and eyes. And they did as much movement as possible jarring left and right to make any sense of where I was or what was around me. To my left a coffee table. Covered with a black and white checkered cloth. With a small vase holding a few ill-conceived roses dangling to the side. Facing a small television that looked to be about fifteen inches. And an old rabbit ear antenna perched on the top. With a rug lying in front of the TV's wooden holder. Decorated with red dots and soft grey outlines for the background. The head of the couch laid to my right with its detail pale and worn. A few scratches here and there with spots that appeared to be more grey than black. Obscure spots that blended into the dull detail. Following my observation it seemed obvious. I was lying in someone's living room (a good Samaritan?) But the peculiar observation was the fact that I didn't hear any footsteps. Not even a mere sign of life in this empty room. As daunted and dull the life of its appearance was it seemed that the hosts appearance captured the mood. Perhaps they were out at the moment, or in another room making good use of hospitality. But not for evil intentions...

So I did the only thing that I could do at that moment- lay in wait. A few minutes later I began to ask if anyone were there. When no answer came I then asked what I was doing there, who brought me to where I was and why... but again no answer. Well with a slight shrug I decided that three times had to be a charm, and asked once more where I was. But moments later nothing.

And as I began to ask yet another time a light bump seemed to shake the floor. Ever so but it was a very odd and peculiar feel to it- as if... as if someone were stuck in the wall itself. And as I began to assume this rather befuddling notion the bump occurred once more.

And again

And yet again growing stronger with each turn.

It seemed to be on the seventh shake that the ground behind the TV appeared to be crumbling. The small crumbs and pebbles of the wall soon began to fall. And I found myself lying in front of what felt to be a massive earthquake! As I laid there hopeless to the events that lay before me the greatest of oddities occurred. Something began to push through the wall! I couldn't believe my eyes. And yet by some unknown circumstance I saw what appeared to be a face piercing through the wallpaper. As that face pushed further and further and the ground all around shook harder. And as it broke though my skin curled assuring me that I was not paralyzed by injury but rather by fear itself. My nightmares became a reality as the face broke through the wall. The face of a hollowed creature of terrifying proportions! With skin as white as the dead with no eyes to fill its sockets. It began to bellow a God forsaken squeal that will forever haunt my very being. I couldn't hold it any longer! I began to scream, and I screamed until I felt that my lungs would die from exhaustion. I shook with all my might but could not move as that monstrosity moved closer to consume me from bottom to top!

I screamed once more... and I woke up. Strange- it was the same room with the same TV standing near me on the same holder with the rabbit ears on top. And I lay on the same black leather couch glancing at the same wooden ceiling. But the cracks and the shaking. They were gone and there was no evidence of anything breaking through the wall. And once more no one was there. As if nothing happened in such a bizarre sequence. But was it only a nightmare, and if it was then how could I have had a nightmare of a room I've never encountered before? The question raced through my mind when I felt a shake. Nothing as threatening as the ones before. But rather the shaking of a poor foundation one would feel when somebody was walking. And as I realized this I cringed in fear once more. I anticipated nothing but the worst on account of my defenseless immobility. The shaking came closer and closer. Whoever- or whatever was coming for that matter seemed to be carrying heavy weight. Oh how I prayed that it was not a giant demon that struck fear into my heart as a child- oh how I prayed indeed. But for once my prayer became a reality as I saw a woman enter the room. She was holding a tray with a hot bowl of what one would assume to be soup as the steam continued to rise from its surface. The entrees of crackers and cheese further enhanced the warm and delicious aroma. The woman looked to be a very kind person. Perhaps in her early thirties with short blonde hair and dark green eyes. With an apron covering her dull colored blue dress. She entered the room and asked if I was feeling better. That she made me a quick meal to recover from my hard hit on the street.

In response I found that I was able to move. And that gesture not only reassured myself but also this kind looking woman. Then without hesitation she placed the tray on the table and helped me to sit up straight. She suggested that I should begin eating at once. It would seem rather odd that a stranger would give such a commanding performance. And it made me smile out of the corky circumstance. As I ate with no hesitation the woman introduced herself. Her name was Siri and she asked me what I was doing out in the middle of the street to begin with. I glanced over to give a quick response of my unfortunate events. Yet I was hypnotized by her ghastly appeal-

She wore no make up, no lipstick and looked to be more ill than in good health. With bone cheeks curling around her pale colored skin as her dark green eyes gazed forward. But as bizarre as her appearance seemed to be I kept my manners as I explained my situation. And after accounting my strange events she shook her head in concern for the kid. She asked me if I knew the boys name and I told her that I was unable to ask in time. But I gave her what descriptions I could. She paused for a moment, then shrugged her shoulders as if pondering who the boy was or if she had seen him before. She once again paused for a few seconds with the expression of deep thought. And as it appeared she was going to say something she tilted her head upward. At this point this obscurity was beginning to drive my patience. And I began to build up enough courage to ask if she knew about any evidence on where I could find the kid. But as I was about to pop my lid Siri jarred her eyes towards me. She stated that she knew nothing about a boy of that description from River Falls, that is a boy that she knew. And after this oddity she looked forward, starring blank at what appeared to be nothing...

After a moment or so I came to wonder if the woman was pondering. She sat there immobile the entire time. At one point I feared that she died. Or that I may have been stuck in another unimaginable nightmare scenario...

At last she turned towards me. She advised that I go to check the police station in the central area of town for information. Of course! The police was the last source I thought of. Making sure that I was up to full mobility I prepared to move my arms to and from my knees. The result was rather soar but it was a relief to be able to move around once again. My legs stretched at a better rate as I prepared to stand. And as I did Siri looked towards me in deep concern. She advised that I should at least get some more rest before I began to head out. I thanked the her for her kind hospitality and for the meal as I stood and made my way to the front door. It was time to confront the small town of River Falls- this time with a full stomach and a clear mind on the situation. The walk from the squeaky couch to the door seemed much longer and more of a struggle than I imagined. My tired body cringed with all its might. And as I at last made my way to that front door I turned around to once again thank Siri for her help.

But I saw that she was no where in sight-

And how odd that I didn't hear a sound coming from the couch or any footsteps. But whatever the reason may have been I decided not to spend my time waiting for an answer. I turned my way towards the door and my attention to the child.

Even as they acted a bit clumsy at first my hand made its way to the doorknob. And I gently turned it-

The old screeching sound was painful to my ears as the door opened with a creaking howl to go with it. And there I saw- the fog still hovered over River Falls. And as heavy as it was before. It was such a peculiar and depressing state of atmosphere. A feeling I never encountered in this calm and peaceful town. But despite the dreary approach I knew I had to find the courage to continue forward- the poor kid's got to be close. But the police station, where's the police station? I started to ask myself, as I couldn't recall the location from heart or memory. The central area of town could mean anything. The downtown section was near the southern end of the center of town. And the business surrounded it all around with old apartment complexes. And street lights, barricaded with old warehouses and home districts. At least that was the foundation that first came to memory. I thought that I should ask Siri about the location as I peered back. But she still wasn't there, and I felt that I could waist no more time in my search. And with that I made my way out the door and back into the madness. The heavy plaque of the fog that haunted River Falls. It continued its sinister pace all around. It creeped its way all around me and made a menacing dance up and down the street.

The echoes commenced in the inner walls of my mind as I took as much effort as I could to concentrate on the sidewalk. There must have been some reasoning in the middle of all the chaos that lay before me. I searched for an open store or a street sign displaying my current location. But hidden by the massive fog I found that I could no longer wisp away the covering with my arms. It seemed to jeer my attempts by steering its way back to where it had covered. And yet the more I tried to wisp it away the more it built right in front of me, and the less I swiped the more it would stay. And so the only logical conclusion I could make was to move forward in caution. To see with my hands and feet as my eyes have become blinded of the surroundings. Yet the more I grasped this concept the more I felt at ease. As if it were becoming second nature as I made my way through the dark jungle of grey fog. It was then a sign appeared in front of me. What exactly it said I couldn't make out it appeared to be a street sign starting with the letter "M". Mulberry Street? From memory it was the only street name that started with an 'M'. I approached the sign even closer. It was Mulberry, but

Mulberry Lane. Was I was thinking of Mulberry Street in one of the high end housing districts? But wherever it may have been I was glad to at least make some progress in this mundane situation. And what's this? I swore I saw something in the fog ahead of me. The outline of someone standing or crouching forward, perhaps looking for something or-
    I cried out to the figure- it had to be the boy!

First Strike

It had to be him. I knew that he must be all right and that everything would... That is...

That is until I began to observe what did not seem to be at all the form of a child. I ran in full spirit but the closer I came the slower my pace. As if my body rejected what lay before me, a basic instinct to... protect myself from harm or danger. But from a child- why was I so willing to approach in danger towards a child? This though echoed in the chorus of my mind. The rhythm which was once sweet and harmonic began to twist and bellow with agony. The tone began to die as I began to feel the skin on my back once more stand on end. The blood coiled in my veins as I came to a complete halt- fear itself has become embodied within my very soul. Even as I could not see what it was in that distant fog the only truth that I knew... This paralyzed reality summoned by such great debts. Unimaginable even in my most horrific nightmares. I somehow knew and felt the terror deep within my heart. My senses perplexed by all the shrilling madness that came from my recent encounters. Somehow I had to hold myself together, to realize the true reality that lie before me and move onward. But this reality... what form and shape have you become? The further I moved the greater the fear... and the more I struggled against my will the greater the insanity became.

I fought to drive onward in my wearied form of mind, with every footstep harder and longer than the last. I swept away at the harsh fog, and glancing at that very shadow that haunted my soul. My arms cried out in horror and I forced my will against its fear. Now I was getting closer. And closer still to this outline I have yet to confront. and As I fought my way forward why was I unwilling to continue? Yet still I continued onward- inch by inch I fought my way, and by tooth and nail I struggled to no end. And it was at that last moment I felt as if my arm would fall from the socket. That my legs would shatter into pieces as I glanced the nightmare that my senses had warned me about. Oh if only I could have listened... if only I could have.

Even with the dense fog I could see there stood before me not a child- no not even near in comparison of a childish figure. It was a creature appearing to have the form of a man. But only the form of one in the sense that it stood on two legs with feet and had two arms with hands. Its posture was far more horrific as the rigid creature bent forward as the shadows once did. It not only bent over but its body twisted. The torso slugged at an angle as the rest of its body shook even on the slightest gesture of movement. As if the innards were tied together by strings. God why did the fog decease at that very moment? As it did before the fog began to wisp away and before me was this... thing. Even a brief glance made my stomach ill, as I could not bear its tragic figure. The disfigured monster did nothing but stare at me, with those horrible eye sockets- good Lord it had no eyes!

The emptied sockets in that twisted skull gave the reflection of neither life nor death. As if damned to wander in the world of purgatory. And even as it had no eyes it stared straight at me... Not making a single movement as its weary chest inhaled and exhaled. A repulsive representation of its shaking body with every breath. Its stretched arms made no hint of movement even as they seemed to be pre cautious. Ready for defense, or worse an attack. At any rate I couldn't bear to observe this monstrosity as I stood there in fear. Unable to move and unable to think of anything beyond the creature that stood before me.

I knew I had to take control of the situation or else my circumstances would become much worse. Somehow I had to fight the horror that stood in embodiment before me. But was it only a figure of my imagination? Was I only in an untold nightmare screaming to return to the real world? Or I was in the real world screaming into the nightmare...

At this point I could not tell as my conscious self began to rebuttal to my current fear. Eager to send a clear message of courage and hope. And how I wanted to respond. Paralyzed by the haunting glare of this soulless monster...

For what seemed like hours it... stood there gazing into my eyes. Those God forsaken sockets that bared no eyes starred strait at me! Could it even see me or understand that someone was only a few feet away? Could it even sense life in that lifeless carcass? That saggy skin and bones that jolted with the pressure of the air inhaled and exhaled? Like a poorly designed bagpipe? The greatest riddle of all- how could I escape this madness? The disgusting sockets. The sickening and grotesque figure wobbling before me. It was all too much for my senses, as I stood paralyzed by fear of reek. The creature then began to lean forward. And his crab-like legs plunged with its ill begotten structure of an upper body in my direction. Its movement was slow and timid. Yet the action brought an even greater horror deep into the debts of my heart. My only defense was to stand there in disbelief. Hoping intervention would occur. And in a world were God seems to be among the dead.

Closer it crept towards me. The circumstances were growing dyer and I found begging for death would be more suiting. It was so close now-

And how much more vile it was to my eyes that I shut them tightly. As I sweat up a storm, the very storm that forced me into this death scenario. And as I clasped my hands together as my arms shook madly-

An unexpected occurrence of circumstances. It caused my twitting and fear to diminish once more. For as I stood with my eyes closed tight the sound of a loud shot rang in my ears. I felt a warm gooey liquid

THE LAKEFRONT 37

dripping on me from head to toe. Something that felt like blood but cold and lifeless like an artificial substance. My curiosity got the best of me as I opened my eyes. I looked and no one was there... the shot must have come from a good distance away as all I could see were the remains of that ghastly creature. Upon first observation I felt that I wanted to vomit all the fear and horror that bellowed within me. Yet I gained renewed courage as I began to yell out to see if anyone was there. A blast of that proportion couldn't have come from a natural source. The smell of gunpowder was beginning to whiff in the air from the dead remains that poured on the street corner.

After I called out an answer soon echoed from a nearby window. The voice of a man, who sounded like he was in his early 30s or late 20s. The voice asked if I was all right and I responded with a resounding yes, thankful that I was alive and well. I then heard footsteps approach but not the same as the creature made. The sound of boots walking from within a building with a wooden floor. A door creaked open, followed by the thumps of boots on the sidewalk. In the distance the shadowy outline of a man holding a weapon came into vision. And the vale soon broke through the befuddled maze and revealed it self to be a man carrying a shotgun. He wore a tailor suit tucked into a pair of rough blue jeans. And he wore a pair of dirty work boots plagued by dirt scum and grease. On his face he wore the smile of a hard worker with polished teeth to match. And with a toothpick on the lower left side of his grinning maniacal smile. His eyes were a blazing blue that seemed to float like clouds in the sky. and his meshed hair seemed to match the charismatic personality as he looked at me, as if without a care in the world.

He had a good look at me before saying that he was glad he hit the creature instead of me. The comment seemed rather mischievous the first time I heard it. But on second thought the awkward statement came as a joke rather than a threat. and I laughed for the first time since I began this tiresome journey. Then he invited me back into his shop so I could clean my self off. And as he made the offer I took up the opportunity without hesitation. Upon my response he gestured for me to move forward. Looking as if someone- or something for that matter- was watching us from afar. He then ducked down and disappeared into the fog. It took only a moment to realize that if I didn't do the same, I would soon find myself in such a horrific predicament. One that haunted me a few minutes earlier. I ducked and made my way left, trying to find the path way of my newly found savior. And his dirty boots left a dark brown track of dust and dirt on the side walk. Crouching low and often times peering from left to right in caution I evaded my way down the path. And it was at last after crawling on all fours that I ran myself into a crooked wooden door. The texture of scratched and decayed plywood, what seemed to be decades old in age. But the site didn't despise me in the least. And I was glad to find a sanctuary for some much needed rest. One I presumed would help to clear my mind about this entire situation.

 I stood in satisfaction and opened the door. Peering inside I made sure that it was the right door to enter. Inside was the same rough looking man who helped me. He was leaning on the wall of an empty supply store near the counter in an odd stance. As if he were trying to relax but felt too tenacious to be at peace. His shotgun was lying on the counter as he held a magnum in hand. Raised upward near his ear as he stood there leaning on the wall. He said I could come in and that the shower was to the right. It took me only a few moments to take a quick warm shower as I dried myself up. And yet another loud blast occurred from the other room. Panicking I yelled to make sure if he was all right. And he responded oddly enough with a jesting laugh. Said he was doing some target practice on some creatures. I dressed myself and made my way back into the main room. The man stood near the window, looking down on what appeared to be yet another carcass of those creatures. He peered towards me and stated that his name was Tim, and he looked back to the window as if nothing happened. For a few moments he stood there as if I wasn't even there. And if that wasn't bizarre enough Tim began to back up and bumped into me, as if he had forgot that I was there . He almost jumped but smiled as he saw me. Said that he often times forgets when company comes around to his store these days. What with all the creatures luring around. The curiosity of these things sparked new interest in me. And I was about to ask about them-

Then he mentioned the reason why he stands in front of the window. He swears he sees a few people out there every now and then. And he's not going to let them fall prey to some spawns lurking around town...

But how could I forget? The kid's still out there, and what's worse is that these creatures are out there too! I came to my senses as I immediately asked if he saw or knew about any boys who may have made their way around here. To this question Tim glared out the window for a moment and scratched his head with his gun. He turned around towards me and said he didn't think he saw a kid out there. That he was usually watching the streets all day and if he were to see a kid that I would be the first to know about it. It wasn't much help but I thanked him anyway. And as I thanked him he suggested that I should go and speak to the sheriff about any missing people in town. To this resounding information I thanked Tim for his tip and asked where the sheriff's office was. He said it was south of here near the plaza center- of course! The memory once again struck my dumbfounded intellect on the locations around town. And I realized that I was in the center of River Falls. Once again I thanked Tim for his hospitality as I began to thrust my way into the darkness. Now with a more confident and mindful approach- but as I made hast he grabbed my arm with a tight squeeze. I looked back at him and for the first time I saw there was a feeling of deep concern in Tim's eyes. Or remorse as it was hard to tell from a man who seemed to laugh at the very gates of Hell. He handed me what appeared to be a colt pistol and he said in a generous tone to be careful out there. And he gave a grim smile saying he didn't want to dig up my dead carcass on the side of the road.

As odd as his caution sounded I told him I would be careful out there. Tim made his way back into the shop and I stood there feeling perplexed about the situation. Yet I shook it off, thinking to myself that I didn't want Tim to come out and clean up my dead carcass...

Eye of the Storm

The scenery was beginning to clear now. The deathly fog made its retreat as I moved forward in search of the police station. As if my newly found confidence crippled its strength. As I peered left and right in caution I could still notice the fog. I moved forward it still blocked most of my visible clearance. And I saw what appeared to be shadows of lurching creatures. Or what I believed to be lurching. As there seemed to be others that bent. As if its spinal cord had snapped at its center but cursed to wander and feel the agony. Usually the only thing on my mind would be the boy's safety. But it shifted towards the needed security from the hand gun Tim gave to me moments earlier. I didn't have much experience on a shooting range. That beyond observing John Wayne films in utter awe during my childhood years. But I felt confident none the less in case of any emergency or threat at hand.

And in the same way that gun brought me much needed confidence it also wavered a sense of caution and fear. there could be innocent people out there, in the same deadlock as I was. The more these thoughts ran in my often curious mind the more I wondered about these creatures. I should have brought the subject up earlier. Tim- he knew that I didn't live in town. That I was here on visit, searching for a child in the mist of what appeared to be the heart and soul of madness. Why didn't he at least give some explanation about these things luring in the streets and shadows? The more I asked. I couldn't help but come to a conclusion. That nothing in what appeared to be a God forsaken town of my childhood. None of it contained rationality. No, I dare so there was no reality to this place- this infinite madhouse of horror...

There's no time for questions! Another creature began its freighting waltz in my direction. I stood in awe and terror as the figures black outline in the fog. It grew larger and larger with each luring step forward. It grew from the size of a small man to the monumental size of a horrific giant. And my feet turned to stone in fear of this unknown abolishment. As I starred in terror my hand felt its way around the pistol concealed in my pocket. My inner conscious seemed to beg for retribution. The need of justice in wake of what happened to me in town, and what could happen to the child if I couldn't find him. How I wanted to fight back. And now that I had the necessity to take matters into my own hands I felt afraid. Afraid that the shadow was in fact not the shadow I was looking for. Or that it was the wrong figure, the shadow of an innocent bystander like me, or...

Or... no it was too late now. My hand thrust the devil from my pocket and the blazes of Hell came from its tip as my eager fingers pulled the trigger. The smell of the smoke was dark and crisp. It was hard to breath in as I stood there not knowing to be proud, lucky or sorrowful. A large clunk followed the ringing in my ears as I saw the shadow collapse. I made my way forward and I felt that gooey surface on the bottom of my feet. I looked down and it was the blood of that creature. And how relieved I was that it was a monster and not an innocent person that I took down. The further forward I went my feet meet the hard skull of this creature. This grotesque monstrosity with a twisted neck and body. Its chest rattled in two by the bullet that flew from my gun. As I stood there starring at it I was of course frozen in horror at such a vile creation. Yet I found myself heart broken that these things had to exist. As if not killing them would be torture to them. That living was Hell and death was their salvation. The irony perplexed me as I could do nothing but stand there. I must have stood there for at least a minute. And I realized that I was actually sympathizing with this horrendous monster. And I shook my head and told myself to move on- more important matters lie ahead of me.

And once again I made my way through this accursed place. I made caution as I slipped left and right. To and fro from any suspicious shadows that lurked in the distant fog that haunted my soul for so long. If the suspenseful atmosphere didn't kill you than the mutiny would do you over. For it was well over ten minutes (at least it felt that way) since I made my second departure. Yet not one noise came from the fog. An occasional movement of my steps and the random shuffle of feet in the distance. But I swore that I could have heard a pin fall to the ground from a mile away. As if being stuck in this desolate fog wasn't bad enough. Now I was being tortured by the silence of death itself.. But whatever the reason I moved on. And it must have been yet another ten minutes before I saw what appeared to be a very long and narrow shadow. It was different from the others in town. It was playing games with my intellect on whether to once again draw out my weapon in defense.

The decision to move forward. To move without caution before making any attack seemed like the worst case scenario. But looking back at it I thank my collective subconscious for making the right decision. As I made my way forward I saw that the shadow bared no resemblance to a human or creature of any kind. It was very lean and angular, as much as it was tall and motionless. As I moved forward it made no retreat, no advancement of any kind- it stood there. The closer I came, the larger the shadow grew but with no movement at all. Was the 'thing' waiting for me, ready to snatch me up from my foolish intellect? Perhaps it was injured, or better yet dead. Whatever the reason I move forward. And with extreme caution as this thing only continued to grow stronger...

Whatever it was it had to be at least ten feet- no, eleven feet tall, or more. It was so difficult to gather my strength during those moments. I felt that it would be best to run from the dangers and fears of the unknown rather than to face the oblivious truth. One that could be a horror that I have yet to find or imagine in this Hell bent reality. I began to sweat as my knees shook and my skin once more crawled along the tips of my spine. It was the same fear I had from the previous encounters, and in my heart I knew the presence of fear once more. I wanted to run away. I wanted to leave from what lay before me. But I was stuck in a trance as I continued to step foot by foot towards the unknown doom that lurched before me...

I felt a cool sensation creeping down my spine. A chill that surrounded my paralyzed consciousness. But how can it be that I was lying down in this darkly lit room?

A moment ago I was outside near a fogged outline. Making my way to the police station- now it's a deathly atmosphere as I lay on what feels like a cold table. The dim light on the ceiling looks to be going out at any moment now. I either don't have the ability to move or refuse to. And deep in my mind it seemed that the worse was yet to come. I lay there feeling hopeless for the first time since I began my excavation.

As I began an attempt to collect myself I heard a familiar sound of steps...

Echoes as they soon began to die away. It was a moment later that the same sounds returned; only this time the sound came closer and closer. I did my best to turn my head but I somehow couldn't move. Or at least not enough to observe what was making the noise that was approaching. As it came closer I heard a kind female voice asking if I felt alright and not to be scared. The voice gave me a sigh of relief as I continued laying there. The steps came to a halt and there was an eerie pause. As if the voice had died in the air...

And I felt that all was lost. What I interpreted as a glimpse of hope vanished. And the more I thought about it the more it seemed to be a less fortunate circumstance. It could have been another monster after all...

Even as I couldn't move I did all that I could to get some sort of gesture working in my-

Good God! As I had presumed that I was alone a woman appeared in front of my eyes! From where she came from I can't guess, as if she appeared from mid air. And what was even more suspicious of the peculiar haunting was her appearance. I could have sworn that I was looking at Siri whom I met earlier. The same dull expression on her pale face and withered body as she stood wearing a police outfit. As if she was the sheriff all along. But as I was beginning to assume all the evidence she began putting on latex gloves- but why? She then began to say something but everything was mute. I couldn't read lip but it seemed like she was talking to some one else, as if she wasn't alone in the room- but who?

I was pondering over this complexity I heard my voice in the back of my mind. It asked her about the police station, and implying that she was Siri from whom I met earlier in her house. I thanked her for her hospitality. But what was more shocking was the fact that I heard a response from her. But not from her physical self but once more in the dark corridors of my mind. She was speaking something different as her voice in my head started with a light laugh... and ended with a statement. Saying that she was Siri's twin sister Iris. Her sister was a housemaid who works for the community. That she is one of the head sheriffs in River Falls, and has been for the past 9 years. And as the voice spoke in my head Iris looked towards me with a look that appeared to be one of contempt. Or one of guilt or sorrow- it was hard to describe exactly what was on her mind. Especially as I was hearing her voice in mine. It was the kind of moment where you wish you could read lips. But you knew later on you would come to regret knowing everyone's business. A double edged sword...

The dialog in the inner corners of my mind commenced. And I asked Iris what she knew about the town's layout and its inhabitants. As the voices spoke the Iris before me appeared to be putting on a glove.

What appeared to be a latex glove as she put on a surgical mask over her dully-colored mouth. I felt my body yearning to flinch away from this unknown circumstance. But I couldn't move, no matter how hard I tried to struggle against it. My inner voice then began talking about the incident. About finding the boy and getting into the embarrassing car wreck, and why I was stranded in the middle of town. The women in front of me then lurched her head towards the left- as if- as if someone, or something was coming? The voice of Iris spoke once more. It told me that she found the experience and the circumstance unfortunate. That she hasn't seen any children out and about in this area today.

Her head then turned back to me with a look of bittersweet confidence, and I felt a soft beating in my heart. Very small at first but it began to grow- and grow- and grow. But the beating- it wasn't the heart beating. It was-

By God- it was from the floor.

And Iris responded deep in the corridors. Said that she would first investigate any nearby townsfolk. And to ask nearby businesses that were nearby. In the meantime she said she would keep an eye out and make some phone calls to the locals. Keep in touch with them, make a police report and keep an eye out on the situation. Even as the beating grew the voice gave me confidence for my journey, even into this unknown terror.

Hope was born once more in my inner soul. Yet the candle began to wither as the lights began to dim... Fear and superstition was once again within me. Iris's voice called out once more but I couldn't hear her very well. I saw what appeared to be a dark shadow luring towards me... the closer it came the more the fear grew within me, to the point of insanity it grew. Her voice continued, speaking something about an item to help me. Or a hint, but the suspense was beginning to induce me as the shadow came closer. Once again the horror I once knew took over every shred of my dignity... As I looked in fear, it was once again... those red eyes! Those peering red eyes haunted me from the deathly sockets from the man's appearance. I wanted to scream. I wanted to scream until my lungs could not bear the exhaustion. And would wither away as I lay there helpless and immobile. And he pulled out a scalping knife- a scalping knife! How I wanted to scream in agony, and how I wanted to end this suffering. Was there no end to this madness?

My voice screamed! And I found myself standing once more... in front of the mysterious outline that lay behind the overcast of fog... But how could it be? I peered left and right but I was standing on my own two feet as I was a few moments ago. And the fog was dying out once more, and I saw the figure before me- a sign for the police station. And as I stood there bewildered I felt something in my pocket. I felt inside and to my surprise I pulled it out- why it was... a map of the town.

Seven

And there it was- right before my very eyes, in my shaking hands of discontent and delusion. How was it that a map appeared within my pocket? Was I indeed in that foul and hallow place, or what it all a mere misperception of talking to Iris in the sheriff's office? Injured by one of those monsters? And treated after I spoke to her, losing my consciousness along the way?

As I stood there in disbelief the questions kept ringing in my ears. I was unable to collect myself from such a haunting a bizarre occurrence. And those red eyes... good God of Heaven it had to be those red eyes. No matter how hard I tried to escape them I could not bear to see its presence.

Now as the dreaded and ongoing nightmare... that forbidding vigilance began to stalk me once more. Another tall and dark shadow started to appear in the fog. It was small at first. Barley noticeable as I looked past the crudely arranged police station sign. Yet it grew, and with massive proportions. So much that I almost screamed in fright, as I did not wish to be in harms way, or upon death's door. I almost grabbed my gun but hesitated. Instead I make a quick dash across the street where a street lantern was. The fog hovered around its heavenly presence, seeing to reckon itself as an angelic beam of light. One to guide those in their troubled ways. Its presence was more than welcome. And I darted with what courage I could muster within my discouraged soul.

Its luminance bestowed a new sense of hope within me and I could feel my strength and determination grow instantly, and I perhaps for the first time in what seemed to be ages I felt confident in myself and my mission- but also at that moment I decided not to become too arrogant, knowing just how bizarre and conflicted this malevolent town that I once called my home has become. It is perhaps with true courage and determination comes wisdom as I cautiously made my way forward. I saw strange shadows of luring arms and twisted skulls in the distance and as much as my beating heart wished to I refused to stop or to fire madly into the darkness. The only motif that I carried was to keep moving forward, and even as the fog was dreading further away the horizon was still as thickly casted as the sky, and what appeared to be nearby buildings and signs only lay as dark shadows haunting the fog.

The further I stepped the more caution I took as I began to hear a strange noise in the distance- its oddly made pitch made me pause for a moment as I felt befuddled by its ghastly echo. It was both haunting and despairing, as if it were someone crying in the emptiness. I felt that I should run towards the source but thankfully my wisdom told me other wise, that it was best to keep moving forward instead of blindly casting myself into an unknown predicament. But the howling commenced- what a bitter sound it was... soon it became unbearable- its once innocent tone seemed to become malevolent, and I could bare it no longer. Truly a child couldn't make such a hideous noise, no matter how impractical the child may be. Being thankful that my wisdom was with me to deter away from such a nuisance I continued forward to that growing shadow ahead of me, logically guessing (and hoping) that it was a sign to a business or perhaps a safe house.

Wait- business', safe houses, homes and stations- they're found on a map. Of course! And as I thought about it I took a glance at the map and made my way from the police station. I remember there was a- restaurant or some kind of business north of the station. So if I am going north, then that can only meant that- the figure ahead of me was the sign for that business! As excited as I was to come to that conclusion I could not and could bear not to lose my calmness. No matter what the situation...

Following all the encounters that have plagued me thus far. I had to be calm in all situations- no matter what circumstance. Still a sigh of relief and gratitude overwhelmed my worried heart as I made my way forward... one step at a time.

One step- and another- and the next step I heard a faint sound the misty air. It sounded like that- that howling from earlier... At first it was weak and damp. But as I made my way forward the sound grew louder, and louder still. It came to the point I made my thirteenth step. That I could no longer bear its vicious and screeching bellowing in what seemed to be a very close location. I peered to the left and right but saw no shadows beyond the one that lay before me. And as that thought entered my mind I began to fear the darkened figure before me. I knew it had to be yet another creature longing to seal my doom. But no- I had to hold myself together; the only way I was going to find that lost child is if I had the courage to find him. Further I made my way.

And as I did the fog began to enclave me, and the distance seemed to have grown further than expected. But I didn't care. I had to move on. Even with the distant sound of horror in the dark. The dispensed atmosphere that was confining me. And beyond such means of torture and despair.

It became harder with each thrust of my legs but further I made myself to this- this thing that lay before me. I had to make it- I had to find out what it was that lay ahead- it was the only way I could make it- the only way I could find the child. The figure was growing bigger, and larger it grew with each step that I made. So large its presence manifested my very conscious as I once more felt the need to run. To flee and never return to this recurring and endless nightmare. Yet the more I longed to run my heart kept pulling me forward, and no matter what I kept following the enlighten. Now was not the time to surrender- or any time; I knew I had to make it- I knew I-

Dear God no...

There in the distance once more I saw it. It was no mere shadow looming in the fog like the one before- rather it was that shadow. How could I forget that? For I could not- its dark and obscure outline of a twisted creature made my skin crawl, and I shook in fear. I felt for the gun in my pocket but my hands trembled, and I could barley find the courage to pull it out. As calm as I could I reminded myself to move forward, even as my feet turned to stone, refusing my command. Yet I progressed, and I looked over to that God forsaken image. Oh how I felt the need more than ever to run away, to hide from the world before me. But the notion preludes to madness- madness I could not return to; I had to move forward and I had to find a way out... somehow.

My only salvation- the dark figure that lay before me. Yet the contradiction of death and suffering seemed to be only a few yards to my left. And unknown danger lying all around me, with the weight of a child's future hanging in the balance. It seemed at times too much for one dreary soul to carry but I know that I must... closer and closer I stepped forward. It was once again an eternity of wretchedness. With each creaking movement I was ever so cautious to not make a single sound. And fearing for my well being... my life.

It was then at long last the dark figure before me took shape. What appeared to be a long and elongated tower, what appeared to be about 13 or 15 feet high. The thought of another sign gave relief. Yet it was the fear of the unknown that begun to shake my very being, and again I wanted to run away. But with that thought the fog began to drift. And a heavy sigh came to my soul. It was a sign for- a restaurant I would suppose. 'The Seven Seas' read the elaborate sign that stood on the metal post. Written on a fish that was glowing a dense green color. Its face looked rather peculiar. As if it were smiling- mocking me with its small white eyes gleaming in the cool fog.

Even as it seemed peculiar I felt relief to see its presence. It became a beacon of hope in a world transfused into a living nightmare. Then came the noise of... footsteps.

It was coming in from behind me... and I began to shake with fear, for I knew all to well the shadow of darkness was making its way to seal my doom. Even as I refused to peer behind me it was no mistake. That it had to be one of those creatures; the hairs on the end of my neck rose in shock and oh how I longed to pull out my gun. Yet if I did... what if it were someone else, or worse yet- what if it were the child I had been looking for? Yet even worse... more of them in the distance? I could stand it no longer. And as fast I ever could I ran and towards the sign, my only salvation from this damned asylum.

The closer I came to the sign a form of a building took shape. And a red colored door stood before me. A red painted door with an open sign dandling to the side. As I turned the knob I decided to have a look at what it was that followed me. I could still hear footsteps- yet as I was still chilled to the bone of what it may be I looked... but nothing. Nothing at all- I peered in all directions and still there was nothing, and the treading died in the wind. With that I looked forward once more and turned the knob, and the door opened with a squealing wail.

It was dim inside with lights hanging from the white ceiling. To my left and right there red tables with mats fit for four. With a decorative chairs to sit in and menus sitting to the side. A restaurant but no one was there. The 'Please Wait to be Seated' sign stood before me near the cashier's drawer as a small carpet laid its way to the tables. The rug itself had writing on it but I didn't know what language it was. A stick looking figure followed by... two square figures, a circle and a figure in a square. What it meant I had no idea - 'Welcome' or 'Have a Nice Day' ? And I was beginning to feel relieved from the surrounding it came once again. It was the footsteps...

THE LAKEFRONT

This time it sounded like it was coming from the swinging door labeled 'Employees Only'. Feeling more confident than ever I stood my ground. Expecting only the worse of circumstances...

At any moment anything could come out that door. I began to feel my hand draw near the gun as the stepping came closer and closer... and I held my position as sweat began to trickle down my forehead. The door swung open and I was ready-

But it was- not a monster at all; in fact it was an Asian woman (and a cute one). She stood there looking a bit startled as I did my best to return to a more calm and normal position. She asked me if I was all right but I didn't immediately answer her, as I felt a bit embarrassed by my actions. But she seemed to get the hint and kindly asked if I wanted anything to eat. I nodded my head, forgetting how long it's been since I've had a full meal. She went to the nearby tray and told me to take a seat. She made her way back into the kitchen. And upon closer observation I saw how elaborate this restaurant was. the colors came into focus and the hanging sculptures brought a sense of life and charm all around. As I sat the sound of foot steps once again made me nervous... But it was the woman once again. And much to my relief as she brought a plate. It was full of steamed rice and cooked fish along with those little ball-shaped foods... What is it? That's right, some sushi. She sat near me with her warm smile and her short cut black hair and green eyes, and said that I should eat up. And of course I began eating and she seemed to happy by my apatite as she began to introduce herself. Yamata is her name, and she owned the restaurant.

Yet even before I could say my name I began to ask her if she had seen a child. As I felt desperate at the moment, or I wasn't very good with talking to women. She was alarmed at my sudden concern and noted that she seemed to notice a child. One who appeared to be wondering outside earlier. I asked when she saw him and it was about 9 minutes ago, and she seemed worried as she asked what was going on. So after telling her about the incident with the car crash. And I could see her become emotional and she looked very worrisome. But as that emotion seemed to burst from her she began to enter what seemed to be a trance of deep thought. I was going to say something but the way she appeared to be in a deep trance stunned me. As if she had entered another state of mind. It's something that one cannot describe with words. A phenomenon that only the eyes can understand.

And as she sat there in what appeared to be a deep thought I couldn't get over how pretty she was. I wanted to say something but I blushed and turned away, afraid she might open her eyes at any moment. Mystified as I was at whatever was occurring before me... I could have sworn I heard a noise coming from another table. It was further than that, for the noise began to grow. Then the noise...

The noise- it stopped. How odd that something so rambunctious would-

But as I looked before me at Yamata something was wrong. Her head lay on the table and she didn't move. In fear that something happened to her I cried out her name, but she said and did nothing. I sat there, for 10 seconds or more- but nothing...

Then the lights! The lights died out, and I found myself shrieking at this odd occurrence as it took me by surprise. But- no... no God- it was those red eyes! In front of me once more it was the red, glowing eyes that have haunted me on my odyssey. And I screamed with terror! The restaurant painted as black as sin, and utter doom and suffering lay right before me. And as the end seemed to be at hand as the lights began to flicker. Slowly at first but soon they came back on... it was a relief to know that-

But where's Yamata?

Happy Times Again

I sat there relieved to find that I was alive and uninjured. But at that same moment my enthusiasm ran thin as I peered all around, shocked not to see Yamata in any direction. But how can she disappear like that? The lights only went out for a few seconds and- Then it came again. The lights began to flicker on and off. And I could feel the sweat building as I grew stiff with fear and braced for the worst. Despite the chaos that ensued all around me I sat there. My heart was full of fear and uncertainty. My hand felt around in my pocket for the gun- I could take no chances from this point on. Not only was the boy's life in question but also so was Yamata's. And I didn't want to blame myself for any unfortunate circumstances.

The lights began to flash madly as I stood on my shaking feet. What courage I could muster was already fleeing. The noise of rumbling and utter madness shook all around, and its echoes haunted my dreary soul. It seemed like eons before my hand finally grabbed the gun concealed in my pocket. And I prepared it for any sudden attacks. The lights continued with its endless waltz of madness. Blinking and stuttering every moment, every second. Time was not on my side, as I had to escape- somehow there had to be an exit nearby. As I began to stand up with hands shaking and hair on end I surveyed the surroundings. The lights danced with a hellish fury, a dance of demonic madness.

And I took a first step forward, determined to make my way out the same way I came in. And so it came that I took another slow step forward. And as I prepared for the next I heard a rumbling from the kitchen area-

So loud that my feet froze in place, as I was unable to think or move. As muted as I was the horror seemed to be stronger than ever. And oddly enough it was the only feeling that gave me the strength to push forward. There came yet another loud boom... this one seemed to be closer and once again I froze in place. My stuttering hands once more longed for the gun, and this time I didn't hesitate. To my surprise I drew the weapon from my pocket and immediately cached it for emergency.

The lights dimmed and flashed all around me. The chaos ensued as fear grew even stronger within my soul. The lights weaved a dance of death and the echoes of doom boomed louder from the kitchen door. I tried to move but I frozen in fear- yet there had to be a way out- I knew there had to be. I could still move my arms and neck, and I peered from left to right trying to make sense of this mayhem. But the lights were flashing, and the surrounding became unorthodox to my memory. I had to keep looking; I had to- I have to make it out alive!

BOOM!

What was that? No... it can't be...I had to find a way!

BOOM!

Again it rang- and louder...

BOOM!

Its articulation became too much for my weary soul. I covered my ears and shut my eyes closed- and how I wished for it to disappear...

.....

But then... it... it seemed to stop. Right at that moment the chaotic racket ceased to exist. And I pulled my hands away from my ears as my eyes opened. Upon first observation it appeared that the dimming and flashing of the lights began to die out. But only slower-

As if the madness was beginning to wither. And I knew what I had to do as I felt for the gun in my pocket. No it was not my hands that uttered the command but for the first time I took action.

THE LAKEFRONT

The visibility was much clearer now. And the entrance appeared to be a few feet to my left. But as relieving as that was I knew I couldn't afford the luxury to let my only guard down. No- not even for a moment should I hesitate to defend myself, now or ever. The darkness always seemed to be hiding behind a veil as the situation became calm. And I didn't want to off guard once more. So I took a bold step forward with gun shaking in hand. Watching as the lights dimmed on and off and waiting for the horror to show itself before me.

My pace became slower and the light died, and in such a haunting manner. And my fear grew faster than my fingers could pull near the trigger. I almost dropped my only means of resistance. But oh how slow the lights seemed to dim...

Soon it was once again black as sin, and I began to feel panic and hysteria creeping up my chilled and remorse spine. The light was beginning to return... slow this time. And it was at that moment I felt... I felt... a slight and cold whiff of air on my neck. My body froze from the chill and I dared not look to see where it was coming from. As if... something-

Oh God! I made a mad dash for the door ahead- I wanted to scream in terror but found myself muted from the encounter. I made myself to what appeared to be the front door, colored in dim red as the light began to die once more. I felt the door's texture and it indeed felt like the front door. Without haste I aimed the gun back from where I came... but as the lights returned- there was nothing. Nothing but coldness and silence; it chilled my bones as I hastened to escape with what bravery I still had. I swung the door open with gun in hand. And once again into the chaos of River Falls. But the fog was disappearing once more, and I could see my way around much better.

The boy is missing- so is Yamata- and as I thought about this I reached for my pocket to find the map. Damn! The map wasn't in my pocket, not even the other as I made a close inspection. It must have fallen out as I made my way out... think... the police station! I had to make my way back to the police station, and they'll be able to search the area. But as I considered this I also came to reality of the situation- what will happen next? What other nightmares must I survive to make my way to save everyone? It seems that the police would be the best choice. Before I try to run into any more horrific perils- even if the one before me is horrific.

So with that I made my way to the police station. This time feeling a bit more relieved and with gun in hand; it's not about the boy or Yamata after all. This time I made a better pace, as I wanted to avoid confrontation all together- but what's this?

The police station... it's gone- but why?

I could have sworn that it was right in this direction. But it seemed to be nowhere in site- as if it vanished into thin air. I tried moving forward but all that lay around me were buildings of small shops and shadows drifting in the fog. But how could it have- of course! The only person who would know about what's going on around here would be Eric. He's the one who knew about the sheriff, and the monsters. If anyone knew about the whereabouts of the townsfolk around here it had to be him.

I dashed towards his shop, knowing exactly where it was from what was once home to the police office. My pace was quick as I felt my confidence and courage beginning to ascend. The shadows all around me danced a horrific chant. An image I knew would haunt me well beyond further expectations. Yet even as I saw this I made my way forward. Never turning back and ceasing to halt as I carried the gun ready for confrontation. The closer I came to his shop the more and more I felt that everything was going to be better. Even with the shadows darting all around me I had more confidence and bravery than I ever had in River Falls.

Almost there- I could see the sign from where I was. Yes! The sign was up ahead. I could see it once more. The old layout of...

By God... oh God...

As I looked upon the sign for his shop my confidence and inner strength once again withered away. Like the pedals of a flower.

It turned out Eric was there. His desecrated body hung on the sign. A crucified image as blood ran from his open mouth with decay. And blood splattered on the sign... his body dangling from what appeared to be a short and tightly attached rope. His gun- it lay beneath him. I stared in horror, as I could not imagine what would have caused this to happen. What could have warped his already twisted image on life into a catastrophic means to end it all. This must be the greatest of horrors that I have encountered in this Hell infested nightmare. A nightmare I could not awake from.

I looked once again. And noticed what appeared to be marks of fangs or claws on his already beaten and bloodied shirt. It would seem that he no longer had the will to keep fighting, and I turned in pity at the gruesome sight. But I found my conclusion to be too rational. Too soon as I remembered those ghastly marks of decay and suffering marked on his bloody chest. If I had looked once more I would have become sick that very moment. It would seem that he did not easily give up- no, but rather went down as the unsung hero. But the hanging- are these creatures capable of actually using a rope to kill? If that was the case then it seemed that my circumstances were beginning to wither... yet once more in what was beginning to become a much more dark and bleak situation...

I began to panic- all the horrible possibilities. All the horrible outcomes that these things could be capable of performing- and I was out here. Alone... alone I say. I felt for the gun as my shaking hands drew it out in the best way presented in such a state of paranoia. The depths of madness lurched my weakened soul as it did so many times before. The hair on the back of my neck leap in fear; my knees shook harder than my uncontrollable hands. And the air- oh the air. The breeze was as cold as winter, and everything seemed to have died all around me, as I was the only victim left alive. I began to breath heavily and tried to control myself, but I found no means of control left in my shattered being. I knew I had to escape- I had to move. But how could I as my feet felt like blocks of cement, and my spirit weaving further into the decent of chaos? But deep down I- I knew I needed to, and had to move...

The shadows! Somehow they heard the cries of my craven soul. And I noticed its movement becoming more active... moving closer as the outline grew in size. At first it seemed to be so small, but soon it scaled, and it was as large as the building itself!

And as my spirit called for mercy from the insanity I drew the gun forward. The ammo full and my finger on the trigger. There could be no more running- I had to take my stand. I must take one- you won't have to collect my dead carcass, Eric!

I squeezed the trigger without hesitation. Not even acknowledging the consequences of my action.

An inner demon that woke up within me at that moment? I continued to fire the gun into the shadows that had haunted me all this time. It gave a sense of satisfaction as I took action. Yet not enough to distract me from keeping my aim straight forward. Even as my hands shook the whole time as sweat dripped down my forehead.

One by one I heard bodies collapsing to the ground. Then came the sudden urge to escape from what once seemed to be a safe haven. The only path that came to mind was back from where I came. It would seem best to return to the Seven Seas, to see if Yamata may have returned unharmed. Even as I stood there worried of the situation her safety became the most important thing on my mind. I couldn't put my finger on it.. but she seemed to be very important, despite the fact that we met only for what seemed to be moments ago. But for whatever the reason my mind and heart seemed to be set on the same destination.

The shadows still appeared on all sides. But now things were different... they no longer haunted me the way they did as I found myself to be the new predator in this cunning game of survival.

THE LAKEFRONT

I made my way- I knew exactly where I had to go, and my steady pace continued without hesitation. The shadows continued to mock me as they made their maddening promenade all around me. At times I wanted to stop once more and deliver another blow from the bullet's edge. But deep down inside I knew that I had to hold back my fury- there were more important matters to attend to. And miles to go before I sleep- do you hear me Eric? And miles to go before I sleep...

Bread

Steady now. I had to keep myself under full control. But at times it seemed rather difficult knowing how audacious I had become. The shadows continued to mock me. But I knew better than to be defined by its image. The never ending madness and obscene presence that once shook my very fiber. It seemed that I teased them, that they were running in terror from my haunted presence. It was a rather good-malevolent feeling, even. Not that I wanted to practice mischief... the feeling that I could once again have a smile on my face brought back a sense of confidence and good spirit.

Of course even with this seldom charm I knew my true intentions lay further ahead of me. Yamata had to be safe and sound, somewhere- and how could I forget the boy? Bless his heart, he must be out there somewhere, and I would hope that somewhere is a safe haven. But wherever he is I'm going to find him- no matter what. Nothing is going to stop me now-

Not even you- those damn shadows are lurching their way once more. Without hesitation I drew my gun. It felt like it had enough ammo to last a few more shots if necessary. But I shouldn't waist them on wandering spirits. I needed to be quick, calm... and careful. I had to take a few heavy breaths of air in and out of my lungs as I passed through this forsaken labyrinth. The shadows grew and shrunk. Off and on- it seemed they were more confused. Or conflicted by something. I couldn't put my finger on it and I didn't have the time to spare, as I was careful not to let my mind wander into such doubts. Even with their random and often suggestive movement I had to stay

THE LAKEFRONT 63

focused. on the path aheaps now more than ever if I wanted to not only help others... but myself.

The shadows again tried to intimidate me as they began to grow once more. And an eerie quiver began to crawl up my spine. A moment of doubt growing within my consciousness. But I shook it away with all my might, knowing it was nothing more than the raven tapping at my front door. I remained in a calm and steady mindset. And I knew that the Seven Seas had to be close from my location- a little ways northward and to the left. With every step I grew more cautious of my surroundings. Not knowing who (or what) would manifest itself from the layered abyss that surrounded me.

I had to be there by now. This part of town was so familiar to me from my childhood. And I was certain of its surroundings moments ago after making my escape. It felt like it was only a few more steps- it had to be there, I knew it. So I kept walking- but... nothing. I lost my track by a few paces? I paused for a moment and glanced south to determine what I missed. And I came to the conclusion to retrace my steps- but again I found nothing... as if it... disappeared.

It seemed like nonsense... But then again nothing seemed to make sense in this mad world. This dark metamorphosis of reality. One that has already driven my mind to the edge of insanity too many times. So as there was no reasoning in this realm I felt that it was best to retreat back to the shop. Hoping to find some lead way or clue to the whereabouts of Yamata and the child. All hope was not lost- all sanity is.

Again I made my way back and forth. Hoping that the restaurant would appear before my eyes. That I for once was the fault of all this chaos- but nothing.

Not surprised I finally turned back, and with a soft sigh made my way to Tim's shop. The only thing I could do now was hope for the best. More than anything this place needed hope, for my sake more than anything else. And so off I went and- what was that in the distance? I didn't notice it before but- but it appeared to be some sort of... shape, a structure or building. I stood bewildered by this odd occurrence. I checked this area a good number of times, but how- and where- did the shadow appear from? My intellect boggled as I stood there, puzzled and wondering what it could be in the distance. Another trap? But it can't be. And even if it was the valor flowing through my blood was stronger than it had ever been. It left me to one choice and one choice only. To excavate whatever the mysterious object or construction was. And my heart began to beat faster. So exhilarated by this courage and determination.

I thrust my legs forward and they felt as light as a feather. I made my way to the mysterious figure as I kept both eyes peering from left to right. Suspicious of lurking shadows that may appear. They seemed to once more dance in madness all around. But I kept myself together as I knew they were only trying to distract my way. And the more I concentrated on making my way the closer I felt to the... building? It indeed appeared to be a building standing a little ways off in the distance. But how could this be? I knew I had to have checked the area. At least two or three times; yet somehow there seemed to be a building within site, right before my eyes. As I began to realize this odd phenomenon my pace became slower and slower. And I stopped for a moment as I shook my head in disbelief. Trying to collect myself from its strange and sudden presence. I tried to shake it off once more but it seemed to keep coming back, not giving up on my valiant effort to stand ground.

As I began to move I felt- different. The assurance that I once had. It seemed to be fading away as I realized that I was once again alone. In an unknown place that... seems to reimagine itself. The fear grew once more, but if only a little.

And it crept up my spine... with a chilling spell that came from its touch; once again I began to feel unsure of my path and of my safety. I wanted to escape from it all. My feet turned to blocks of hard

THE LAKEFRONT

cement and I found my body suspended from movement. I began to see a different shadow growing from the distance. And the shadows in the fog... they knew my fear... and they grew.

I had to take action, so I mustered all the courage, all the fight that I could in my weakening soul and made my way forward. It was very slow at first. The rising shadows descending upon me. They wreaked nothing more than the unbearable thought of certain doom and despair. Harder I fought as I made my way forward to the unknown image that was my only salvation. The maddening chaos grew all around me- I had to hurry my pace! Even as it seemed slow I gained momentum, and I felt my pace beginning to grow stronger. Lord knows how frightened I was, how I wanted to escape from it wall, or to wait for the madness to end me once and for all. Even with gun in hand I felt no assurance from its presence- my hands too cowardice to draw the trigger. Yet as the fear grew inside of me the pace of my motion grew as well, a reaction towards my causation. Hoping my conscious was right I continued my way forward, even as the shadows grew larger still...

It was like an abyss closing in on me, ready to swallow everything in its trap- a spider on its web. And the shadows grew so high that the light began to dim. Only few shades remained as my pace grew faster in fear of the occurrence. Larger still they grew, higher than the sky itself and so dismal was my path. I looked behind me to find the way that I came. But it was swallowed by the darkness, and I feared that I was the next to fall victim to its scheme. Faster than ever my pace moved forward. Running into blackness I had no other way to turn. Uncertain of which way was forward, or left or right as the darkness encumbered all paths. This- this had to be the end...

And as I ran there was... something out there. That something I did not know. But it seemed to be a dim light, or someone breaking through the cataclysm. And as I saw it I ran faster, knowing it was my only hope of escape from the shadows- by virtue or damnation. My pace was faster, and the darkness concealed all around me as the light became dimmer with each moment. I exceeded my greatest zenith, and my body felt the pain like a ton of bricks. I didn't- I couldn't slow down. No, not now! The light was growing dimmer still, and I began to lose my breath with each thump from my aching feet on the ground. And the light... The light was dying. And I panicked as I thrust myself towards the closing gap. And I felt suspended in that moment for times beyond eternity.

Yet as I seemed to be thrusting towards the grim shadows I heard something. As if it were a voice... Very soft at first, but it grew; someone was calling for me? Who I didn't know, but the voice seemed to be familiar. I could notice it as I ran as fast as my beating heart could allow. Slowing down even for the slightest moment would seal my doom. But there was that opening once again... it was that small gleam of light, right in front of me. The distance appeared to be as far as it was a moment ago. And no matter how hard I tried I couldn't seem to inch closer. But what haunted me was its strange diamond shape that began to form... Metamorphosing into a peculiar shape as the luminosity began to expand. And with it came the mysterious voice- the same voice from before called for me. It asked if I was all right; it said that I needed to wake up. But how could I wake? Am I not already awake? Am I not-

The light flashed and the echoes died, and I felt the warm mattress cushioning my aching body. As I woke the first thing I noticed was the soft woolen blanket covering me. The ceiling had the emblem of a lamb lying in green pastures, surrounded by pine trees and autumn leaves. The sight of this magnificent work of art perplexed my senses. And I felt comforted from its heavenly presentation. It gave me reassurance as I lay there, feeling a bit of relief- this was all a nightmare after all. It had to be as I began to feel more strength return. And I looked around astonished as I found myself lying on the couch of our old home- why yes it was! The old couch my mother brought with us when we moved to River Falls, along with the mantle and the old rocking chair! Why yes they were all sitting next to the couch, the mantle to the left and chair on the right- as it always has been.

 And all the decorations and porcelain dolls, the hamper, the rug- it was as I had remembered. And as I made these wonderful observations... there was something that disturbed my senses. A peculiar smell... it was coming from the kitchen. I had enough strength to stand on both feet (how sudden it seemed) as I began to make my way to this strange aroma. Walking to the left and down the hall. I made my way right and found the old familiar kitchen mom used to cook in. Both day and night seemed to live in this tight corridor. And indeed the smell was stronger. And I peered around to find what it was that gave such a powerful redolence- on the table before me was- a piece of bread. I reached out for it as its smell delighted my senses; and as I reached out I felt the sudden sensation that-

 Someone was nudging my arm as I woke up, lying on a chair. A tall, slender man with a hunting hat and vest covering a buttoned shirt stood before me. He asked if I was all right as I jumped from the chair in alarm, but the man told me to calm down. He informed me that he was Ben, the sheriff of River Falls. And how relieved I felt as I told him about the boy. I was starting to explain Yamata's situation when he told me to slow down. That I should get some pastry from next door to help settle my spirit. So he helped me to my feet and showed me to the door, and told me to go left to the Bakery...

 But what about the boy, and... could it be that... was that- Siri in the Bakery shop? I could swear that it was her, even as she wore make-up and appeared to be livelier than before. I made my way in, knowing that she may know more about the whereabouts than anyone else. I ran into the door as I made my way in with anticipation, and I immediately called her name as I asked if she saw the boy yet. She stood there looking puzzled, as if she never met me before. She shook her head in disbelief and asked if she could help me. I asked if she remembered me but her response was a definite no... and I looked at her name tag... Iris.

I apologized and asked if she knew Siri. She explained that she was her twin sister Iris, that Siri was home for the moment. She asked why I was looking for Siri and I explained the entire situation to her. How I came to River Falls, met the boy and Yamata, and how I made my way to her shop. She seemed to be very interested with my story. Her pleasant smile and look was much more soothing than Siri- it brought me a slight sense of comfort. I blushed as I was near the end of my testimony and she said that I should try to contact her once more. That I should deliver a gift for her. She ducked down and came back over the pantry, and what was in her hands startled me- it was a loaf of bread... from my dream. But was it a dream?

Déjà Vu

This peculiar incident had to be more than mere coincidence- or even random luck, whatever it may be. For a moment I felt that it was... that it was a call. Destiny, in some silly way... a form of divine intervention, or a calling of revelation. But for whatever the reason I thanked Iris for her time. And gave a friendly reminder that I would in fact deliver the bread to her sister Siri...

I opened the door, and it made an eerie squeal as its joints cringed forward to open. The sound made my skin crawl- the fear that was haunting me throughout this forsaken town...

The courage that I had found earlier had seemed to be all but extinguished. And I found myself paused in front of the exit. For the first time in a long time I felt unsure of my path and my ability to achieve it. Voices in my head whispered harsh words and lashed out on my innocence. Their sounds became louder and louder. So loud that it came to the point where I dropped the loaf in my arm and fell to the ground on my knees. I covered my ears and wishing to destroy these demonic chants in the inner walls of my mind. Horrible, ghastly sounds ringed in my ear! Voices and screams crying out for death and lust for blood- oh God the torment!

My eyes shut tight as I could feel the rumbles of foot steps rushing to my side. The madness commenced, and I found no way to end the utter chaos. At long last I gave out a loud shout...

And the noises began to die... their cries began to warp out of my mind, and all was quiet. I opened my eyes, and surprised to find that I was no longer in the bakery. Somehow I was outside, with no recollection of leaving the store in the first place. As I stood there- I glanced behind me... and there was no bakery shop. Next to it was the police office but no bakery, as if it vanished... It vanished...

Without any rhyme or reason- it was gone. Nothing made sense in this place- I felt lost once again. With little hope of saving the boy, saving Yamata- from saving myself. The madness entered into my soul. The horror suppressed every fiber of my being as I stood there- I stood there in fear, my knees shaking out of control. I felt as if I had lost all hope. That same hope that brought me courage and strength; how it had grown and how the darkness destroyed it. Standing there I knew I had to do something... but I... what could I do now? My hands shook- my knees rattled- my soul shrunk. And the fog...

It must have heard my cries of despair as it began to emerge from the dark alley and the desolate surroundings. As if it resurrected from the dead...

I was in shock as I found its momentum growing stronger, as if it had fed upon my own spirit. A tear began to fall down my wearisome face as I became one with the darkness. There had to be a way out... how I wanted to find a way out. But all I could do was stand there. And shaking in horror from what was once more the dawn of a never ending nightmare. A horrid phantasm I could find no end to... No, there had to be a way out- I made it this far and I can't give up now! Even as the darkness peers sharper and blacker than the deadliest of sin, there had to be a way out.

And it was then I remembered the loaf of bread- they must be trying to stop me. Gazing upon its warm, rough texture it must have... something related to all this- but what, and why I could not answer. But this much I knew- I had to deliver it and I had to deliver it now. For whatever reason I had to take this bread, out into the unknown savagery of this place I once lived. A place I once loved. So I did the impossible- I took one step forward towards the street. The fog commenced all around- as I suspected. Another step as the mist began its waltz of madness. The third brought it to a slight halt as I preyed on the situation. My steps became faster, but still in caution and guided by my fears as I peered all over. Careful not to find any watchers in my sight...

The skin- the hairs all stood on end as I held the bread with all my life, knowing that it depended on it. Like a newborn child I was in danger from everything around me. I had no immunity to the darkness- even the slightest mistake would cost me everything. I crept my way forward onto the street with what strength I could use. My feet felt like heavy cement blocks dragging from weighing hundreds of pounds. It was slower still as my stubborn ambitions worked even harder to fight my selfishness. To hide from all that surrounded me. The fog seemed to mock me as I heard what seemed to be a hissing sound in the air. It seemed very faint but was there never the less. Heckles continued all around me, ever so soft and never growing. It knew of my intentions and my emotional state as I continued to struggle forward.

My pace- it somehow grew. Even as slow as it seemed I knew that it was growing. My feet's weight decreased, turning from the hardened cement back into flesh once more. I made my way forward, knowing that anyone or anything could be luring me to my doom. My progress exceeded my bewildered expectations as I made my way forward. Those ghastly red eyes beset on me once more...

Deep from within the fog there shape took form, as they did in the past. As horrified as I was by their unannounced return I knew I had to move. I could take no other action and I did my best to shake away any shroud of doubt in my bewildered mind.

Although the gleaming of their eyes appeared I never once saw the creatures luring away from the fog. As if they were mocking me, waiting for me... to make their next strike, or to see me fall, and swoop in like the vulture on the dead. I began to worry once this thought came to mind. Yet it seemed to be an advantage on my account. Their distance provided me the opportunity to advance onward on my journey. And with little to no encounters from these 'watchers'. Thus once more I made up my mind and continued moving forward. And my feet were beginning to grow in pace.

I came to a point where my surroundings seemed to be- obsolete. Vanquished by the fog as its veil covered those hideous beasts. Stopping for a moment I looked behind as I saw nothing but fog- ahead of me was the same circumstance. Afraid that I had lost my path I felt the need to retrace my steps. But deep down it had to be a temptation into the bowels of death, even damnation itself. But then... could it be that... that this fog... is...

The two glaring red beams to my far left grew in size- and my heart began to race. The sweat ran down my body, entombing what courage I had- like a candle in the dark wind. I had to run! I must leave, and if I didn't only God knows what would happen...

And my pace began to wither away as the leaves of autumn, and it rotted to a slow pace as those red eyes came closer still. The larger they grew it seemed the slower I became. But despite the greatest of my efforts it seemed that I could not escape ultimate doom. I couldn't let it end like this. And with what strength, what courage I had left in my feeble soul I exhausted every ounce I could. At last it began to pay off, as my pace was beginning to pick up. As hard as it was I bared every inch of my vigor to the point I felt that I would faint from exhaustion. And yet my pace wasn't that fast. But oh how I wished it was. Now the red eyes began to form a grotesque figure around it. And the horror that I feared to encounter approached at a much faster rate... With great haste I pushed all my energy into my stride, attempting to run.

It seemed to be a game of cat and mouse- predator and prey- demon and soul. The harder I pushed the nearer it seemed to be, and the further I traveled it seemed that I barley moved forward. This demon had the upper hand, but how I hoped for a miracle at that moment. But knowing my surroundings all too well I didn't hesitate to keep moving. Even as all hope seemed out my precious grasp. It was no time to wait for a miracle to happen- they did not exist in this town... not anymore. I began to realize this the more and more, as I began to hear a vague sound approaching. It was very light at first, barley caught by the deathly silence of the surrounding fog. I looked in its direction- and miracles died within my lifeless soul. There, before me it stood...

It was that creature once again- lumbering around with neither rhyme nor reason. Its only path seemed to be forward, but it continued to sway left and right. As if denying its preordained path and logic. For a moment I felt compassion for such an unfortunate fate. But my good will faded away as horror began to creep up my spine. The chill of the air caught the attention of my breathless mouth as I began to pant.

My shaking hands attempted to reach into my pocket- the gun had to be there. They shook as I could not control the tremors of my exhausted soul. It seemed that my heart was beating so fast that it would collapse at any given moment- but somehow there had to be a way. With all my might I tried to control them...

It... It's coming closer! By God what ghastly eyes!

At last I grasped an object in the lower pocket, yet my hands jolted in fear...

Closer the creature came... What vile ears it had!

I took hold of the gun, and desperately drew it out; my only will to take it down once and for all...

It opened its mouth- such a horrifying site I have never seen!

As if the abyss of Hell opened right before me. And I screamed in horror as damnation spewed from its deafening howl. I drew the gun to shoot- and I watched in terror as it slipped from my hands. It fell. And it fell forever, as I was powerless to stop it from crashing on the harsh, dark pavement. As I glanced into this dark creature something told me to run. And without hesitation I moved as fast as I could, as far away as I could. Without even knowing where I was heading I began a fast pace away from this... creature. Faster and faster I moved as my pace darted into the unknown. Beyond the surrounding fog and the fear of death itself.

As the disparity grew within my heart the faster my pace became, knowing there was no turning back... the abyss behind me as my salvation hid in the distant unknown. How fast I was running I will never know. I seem to bolt past blankets of fog as I saw those sinful red eyes starring from all corners in this labyrinth of decay. Faster and faster still- there seemed to be no end to the madness as my surroundings became a distant blur. Faster and faster- I could not control my pace! I could not stop my speed as everything flew before my obscure vision, and it all became a horrific blur of chaos. I had no control of my speed and the ineffability grew within the madness.... I have to stop! I have to stop!

And it was at that moment- the disarray of shadows and blazing speed came to a sudden holt. But... but how, and why? I stood there more perplexed than grateful. My weary mentality once again questioned. But what startled me the most was- the house!

There it was! Siri's house stood before me. And as that came to thought I noticed that the loaf of bread I was carrying was gone. But it didn't seem to matter as I made my way to the front door. I knocked... And knocked... once more, but nothing. Frustration possessed my fear and I banged louder on that decayed door. Yet despite my effort I found nothing, and it seemed all hope lost.

I slouched in defeat as it seemed it was meant to end here, with no more hope... but something caught my dis tainted eye... a letter- a note? I grabbed it from the corner of the window and unfolded its grotesque texture-

'Iris-

A report on the radio announced that there was a car crash about half a mile from town. They say a child is near the accident. And his whereabouts are unknown- he might be near the vehicle, and I doubt he traveled too far. Since I'm out for the moment leave the bread near my window. Love you!- Siri'

All's Well That Ends Well

This jarring revelation left me in awe. Both of relief and stupidity. Comforted that the kid was all right but stupefied by my own action of leaving him by himself. But his... himself! If he really is out there alone... and those creatures... they're...

I jumped as I donned the reality of the situation. Above all else his protection had to be my main priority, his safety was more in danger than mine could have been. Even through all the horrors and the bellows of Hell I have travelled. Even through all the trials and tribulations. And the depths of pain and agony. I could not for one moment begin to even imagine how he must feel being alone in this God forsaken wasteland.

How foolish I have become- and at that the note slipped from my hand, dismayed by my sudden circumstance. I turned left and right, hoping to find my way as the dense fog continued to grow from the dark mist. They must be working to torment me once more. And I must above all else find what courage I can muster in this manifestation of hell-fire. It was no longer about my safety, as reality manifested my harsh crises. That should never happen, no matter the situation. And I hoped that my foolish actions did not jeopardize the child and his safety. Even with no gun in hand and no loaf of bread on my arm-

I had to find not only the strength. The determination to move forward. To fight tooth and nail through this morbid landscape. And as I once did before I reaped what little courage my soul had harvest, gathering what breath my weary lungs could consume... And I stepped into damnation- but my mind cried to turn away, weary of the haunting and the remorse I have come to suffer.

I set away its pitiless cries and ignorance as I waltzed into the menace that lay before me- and how I knew it desired to swallow me whole, and how I felt my body shake as it did so many times before... And oh how my inner mind cried in fear... To run away and never return to this damned labyrinth.

The first step drew a growing mist. The second shook as the mist grew larger still. And the third became hesitant as my mind began to sly away from the unknown that lay all around me. For whatever the reason- be it courage or dumb founded instinct I fought with all my might. I moved onward into the darkness as I felt more and more uncertain with each creep. Fog commenced from all sides as I took as much time as I could. Exhaling and inhaling what breath my wearisome self could take. And prolonged into the depths of the fog and despair, wishing only for my doom. But... no, no it couldn't be...

Matters turned to the worst as I once again fathomed the glowing red eyes in the distance. They returned once more to seal my doom...

I saw in horror as those ghastly figures lurched through the fog on all sides. Not swaying from left to right but from the ground, and some even taller than the ones that manifested my soul. Now there was no gun. And no way to defend myself from these watchers in the distance. I felt remorse inflate from within my heart. Knowing I had little to no chance of not only saving myself but the poor boy whom I've brought into this great peril. Yet it was no time for remorse as they lured closer still. Their grotesque shape and form emerged from the thickness. Like a venomous insect had sucked the precious life of a dying flower...

But yet my heart plead to move forward even as my spirit began to die. Withering away with each slow and cautious step I took.

One of the shadows seemed to come closer still. And I saw a most grotesque shape emerge before my eyes. My lungs collapsed as I held in the urge to scream in terror, swallowing my pride as it came closer. My palms, my forehead...

Every part of me drowned in sweat, shaking as I held back the temptation to run away. It was the first time that I was facing what was fear... An event that shook the very fabric of my soul. My being began to loose control of confidence and the will to carry on. Now it was all on the line of a thread with death heading into my path. It only seemed to be a matter of time before the end would stretch its grisly hands upon me and seal my fate. The malevolence grew stronger still...

Closer it came, and the closer it came the thinner its shape- one that I had not seen in this distant fog. A slight sigh of relief grew within me. But became inanimate as I reminded myself to stay afoot and act with caution. Yet there seemed to be a slight sensation of calmness stirring from within. But my heart hardened remembering to never lower my guard...

And the shape...

It was...

Warm...

And...

It was...

Despite fighting it I could not for the likes of me conceal a sense of hope. Growing, and slower still as I walked realizing the danger that lay before my weary eyes. Why was I feeling this way? Has my soul finally accepted the abyss and wishes to return to the darkness?

And it approached me... this time at a faster pace, and it grew in size. Was it a gratifying figure that came before me? Or could it be my doom approaching to vanquish what such small life and hope lay within my weary self? There where so many questions, so many questions in my mind. I felt as if I was becoming insane from all the voices in my head, all screaming at once as they demanded my response. I desired to run away. But my feet were solid as cement, and I stood facing an undying curse. Will this never stop? But... but why can't I run? It's as if... as if I don't want to run.

And this figure. Why, it was morphing into...

It was less grotesque the closer it approached. And the stones began to melt as I could once again feel my feet- yet I felt no reason to run...

I had to run, but... I didn't. And the shadow came closer still. But I stood there, as if suspecting a miracle. For whatever reason I stood there befuddled by my own coarse of action. And even as I knew death approached me with no way to escape I stood before it- what seemed to be in curiosity... or hope.

And the shadow- it seemed to... loose its shape. And something came into sight- yet it wasn't the bent shape of a creature... but could it be? It came forward at a slow pace. It became more soothing, more appealing. I held my urge to fight back as a small sensation of hope entered my battered soul. The closer it came, the more... familiar it was. And then it revealed its true form... Yamata!

It was her all this time! My perplexed and wounded spirit cried out in joy as she approached. Her worried and cautious expression became a smile of relief as she hurried her way forward. Her slow pace became faster and she threw her arms around me, saying how wonderful it was that I wasn't injured. With no hesitation I asked how she was able to escape with no harm. Yamata seemed to giggle, in joy or relief. And she explained how the restaurant had different openings to the basement. How thankful she was to know every one of them by heart.

To know she had escaped unharmed brought a feeling of joy that was so rare in this other worldly place. And her beautiful smile brought back all the strength and hope that I so needed. Before I could even ask if she was alright she seemed to demand to know about my health. And she somehow seemed more radiant as I gave a response and embraced me once again. And in that moment of serenity, as I held that beautiful women in my arms. And the joy in my heart burst in chorus the child returned to mind. The reality crashed into my cloying dreams. Oh course! That was the whole reason I was still wandering about. And I explained all that I had learned about him and the note that I found. As surprised as she seemed to be with my sudden change in mood. Yamata was fortunate that nothing had happened to him and wanted to join me in my outing. Saying that she had felt somewhat responsible for delaying me in my search. Her reply didn't seem to make sense but I was more than willing to let her join me. Seeing as how a companion would help with so much stress and suffering.

We started into the heavy fog, ever so cautious with each set as I felt more confident than I had ever felt in my life. Even as I heard... but what was that? It seemed to be the sound of... flapping from above us. I paused for the moment, grasping Yamata's arm gesturing for her to do the same. The sound started weak and distant, but it grew...

And it was louder...

And louder...

Louder still as if it were...

Once again I grabbed Yamata's arm as I began to duck down, trying to make sense of this obscure noise. She looked worried as she wrapped her hands around my arm. The sound altered from a flapping noise to a screeching sound as I felt the pressure of the air above me. And that was when I realized that...

I screamed to duck, and I no longer felt Yamata's grasp on my arm. I looked all around me. And as I peered up my confidence altered to a state of disbelief and terror... as a demonic figure flew into the pale sky with Yamata grasped in its grotesque claws...

Dance of the Cherubs

I stared in horror. Immobile and frightened by that ghastly vision in the sky. To even imagine Yamata being in a plight of devastation broke my reckoned heart. But to actually encounter such a gruesome nightmare shattered all expectations. There I was, powerless and weakened as that God forsaken creature flew into the death of the fog. Its distance drew further as I heard a petty cry within my soul. Beckoning to bring salvation from this arch fiend. I once swore to protect those lost in this asylum even as I am lost and afraid. Yet as this cry of justification bellowed from within my weakened heart to touch the very fabric of my soul it was the cry that came from above that nearly rendered my entire being- it was a soft cry for help, and once more...

And Yamata's soft and innocent cry mutated into a coiling and haunting cry of despair and pain. A sound that haunted me unlike any other. But what could I do? The ghastly sound froze every part of me. All I could do was stare in horror as the creature flapped its skeletal wings into the distance. Yet I fought tooth and nail in hope to regain control. May it be that as an act of virtue or pure luck I regained myself and began to move forward. It was slow at first as I seemed to be loosing determination. But I had to fight back, and my pace grew faster with each determined step I took.

And oddly enough, even as I knew without the shadow of a doubt that my pace was progressing faster it seemed as if... As if everything was moving slower. I could see it. Every fabric and trait from the fog, weaving its corse around me in a haunting enchantment. The glare of crimson red dots echoed from the distance. As I looked above I saw those dastardly wings, both flapping as the wind orchestrated to its movement. The bare bone structure of the wings covered by gruesome and decaying skin dis chanted me. In disgust I saw the slow flap of a rotting corpse. And carrying such a divine individual into the inner fabrics of Hell. My heart more than ever cried for justice and redemption yet even its cry was slow and petty.

Has it all at last caught up to me? Has the persistence of the death, the decay and despair that has lead me to this place? That has woven this madness? That has crushed my soul and dragged me towards the depths of the abyss- has it at last caught up to me? My heart beat faster each moment. The horror of feeling every fabric of your body moving. Yet under the realization that you were not advancing- as if time itself was my fate. Even under this macabre I didn't want to just give into the darkness- I didn't want to give up, not now or ever... But why did I care so much for... What was her name? It was all so slow, so mundane to my memory... Why was I sacrificing my life for her? Was it for her protection, or for mine? And the boy? The questions echoed like the church bells on a Sunday- ever so soft...

And I felt cold... So cold. Weak at first but began to become intense at the realization, and yet the bitter cold that seemed to encompass such a dire situation... Had no effect to my body. It felt so odd as I ran, and I knew it was cold but was not. The fog... All around me... It seemed thinner... And I questioned where I was even as my heart knew the truth...

Yamata! I cried out to the sky, bellowing her name and yet not knowing why. Again her name echoed from my mouth as I saw her struggle- and it was then...

A sound from the distance echoed- it was a loud pierce, as it slit its way through the desolate fog. As I ran I could see it's echoes. The fabrics of its remains as it flew forward- the fog rippled on all sides, and I was able to see it. A bullet that was making its way towards the

THE LAKEFRONT

demon. Straight on to the twisted monster- and the creature reared its twisted head towards the lap of the Gods. The end has found its climax, and the certain began to fall upon this abomination. It's eyes grew wildly as the mouth screeched in terror- it was both a site of satisfaction towards salvation and a horrific display of devastation... The bullet ripped the creature asunder as my pace began to wither; I could not escape from such a gruesome site. The fiend began to wither, the limping skin wavering as the bone snapped apart. It seemed to break forever as the sense of satisfaction filled from within.

Yet it was only short lived as all things are in this blissful world- the breaking of the bone caused a chain reaction, slitting away at its once strong grip on Yamata, and my satisfaction quickly and harshly twisted into a reality of fear as she fell... She fell... She fell forever as I swiftly ran towards the fallen angel... And I ran... I ran forever... I seemed so close, and I thrust my arms forward as I knew that I could...

But I...

And she...

And the sound of...

Yet there she was, lying on the ground as I was too late. Yamata hit the concrete. The sound of pain and devastation mirrored from all around. And she lay there hopeless- As I stood there broken.

I rushed to her side as blood dripped from her limbs, laying immobile- how I hope she did not lay lifeless. Quickly I turned her towards me as I held her- even as she was covered with bruises and bathed in blood she was so beautiful to me... Her eyes glimpsed a sign of life as she panted. Peering towards me her aching slowly became a smile... She coughed harshly as she attempted to say something... It was very grim, as if she was attempting to deliver something important but trying to conceal it.

"Ohhh... M-mm... We always... An.... We... We... But jus... Know... I... Loo... I......"

She was slipping away as I sat there feeling hopeless, anguished that I could not save her from such a retched fate, and all I could do was sit there- holding her as tears rained from my eyes... What was she saying to me? What was it?

She became motionless, and she lay there in my arms... Not a breath nor a smile befell from her, and I closed her eyes for the final time. As I cried I took her lifelessness into my arms, embracing her. I have failed to protect her... I have failed to...

But who...

Who is she?

I... I can't remember...

The light piercing from the void. It manifested my entire view. Everything illuminated, blinded it brilliance. And I found myself sitting. Sitting in the middle of what appeared to be a park on a hillside. Surrounded by pine trees and dandy lions with a few rocks sitting on the clean grass. It felt like spring time... the sun was warm and bright...

I sat on a blanket as I heard the chirping of birds as the clouds lay in the blue sky. The trees danced with the wind. And it felt almost too perfect...

Wondering where I was I peered left and right, and I noticed a little girl sitting next to me. She smiled as I sat there in confusion, but cautious not to show my emotions- but how could I be here? and why?

She asked if I wanted a sandwich, and I responded with a resounding yes. Delighted with my response she opened her small basket with her cute tiny hands. She pulled out what appeared to be a peanut butter and jelly sandwich. And she handed it to me, saying that she made it herself. I smiled as I accepted her kind offer, not knowing what to say or do otherwise in my perplexed situation. With the sandwich in hand I took a bite as she watched in delight. As if expecting me to respond in a positive way. It was well made as she smiled seeing me take a second bite, followed by another. She once again felt inside her basket and pulled out a sandwich of her own. I couldn't tell what was in it, only that it had some vegetables inside.

Her tiny hands grasped the sandwich. And she prepared to take a large bite of it, as she almost blushed from preparing to take such a large bite. Yet as she did something... hit her.

Even as there was no force applied to her. She bent over as she dropped her sandwich, and it fell...

It fell for what appeared to be forever. I saw the intricate details of the lettuce and the salmon falling from the wheat bread. The sauce that once covered the inside as they all fell...

And there I was... holding that woman in my arms with tears flowing from my eyes...

But...

But who is she?

Claro De Luna

I have failed- I wanted so badly to protect those who were as lost as I... it was my undoing. Not realizing that I was weak, that I could not be a savior for the lost. And so I sadly left her there, dismayed by my inability to save her- yet the whole reason why I was there... Yes the child. If I could not save this woman- how could I find him as well? I am no hero, and I am not the deliverer, for I am not the man I thought I was. Even he died to the hands of those things... But why can't I remember his name? This woman... I cannot remember, and yet she seemed so significant- the reason seemed to be right in front of my very eyes, yet they were imprisoned...

But by what? It was as if nothing made sense at the moment. Everything lost... vanished into thin air as I stood there perplexed by this occurrence...

"Honey?"

The woman laid there. And glimpse of sunlight pierced into the fog. The once hallowing and retched misery of this place began to wither all around. And the sight became clear, it revealed itself.

And there lay a decayed road that lead its way up a small and steep hillside. A roadway that soon began to reveal itself within the dark chasms of my mind. I inquired toward this newly found discovery, wondering why it had such great significance- again I looked down at the woman with tears in my eyes, and I peered into the distance... There seemed to be something up there, a large object. Larger than a human, perhaps it was something used for protection or... Transportation! Quickly I ran towards the road, and the incline began to grow as I once more recalled the beginning of my journey- I was driving somewhere, and a boy was lost in the rain... I crashed... He somehow disappeared into the unknown... And as I made my way further up a distant outline grew in my mind... A white outline of someone- it was someone- something... Very tall. With no eyes... Yet as this image appeared within I swiftly made my way upward towards that distant object, and as my pace grew I heard a shuffling sound, a very light sound from below... From my pocket. I came to a halt and felt inside... A map. And its destination... lay right ahead of where I stood. This map, it was from... It was. Where was it from, and why did I question its existence?

"Are you all right?"

Yet my destination lay before me, as the steep roadway became flat and twisted to the left. It was all so peculiar, as if I had been here before- yet I could not recall when, or how. Yet I had to be there, for a significant reason. Why else would the map that appeared in my pocket lead me to exactly where... And there it was- A car.

It was ruby red with solid grey tires, shimmering light on its intricate finish. The front smashed into a tree that stood near a harsh curve. For a road that lead towards the mountains in the distance. From the inside there seemed to be a large amount of damage. A wreck that was devastating at its moment and even now- the passengers seat! In it there seemed to be...

"Wake up..."

I ran to the other side and made my way to the passenger door. Quickly I thrust it open, and even as it was unyielding at the first tugs its stubbornness gave into my will- and I found... By God. No... It was- the child. Dead...

His corpse sat there in the seat, scarred all over. No trace of blood, no explanation of such a foul occurrence. It was there- lifeless. Lifeless as I stood there, realizing I was unable to change his fate- that death had once more beaten me. Once more I have failed... I couldn't bear the consequence as I stood in agony at such a tragic sight. Why did everyone have to die? Why? My anguish materialized into anger. Into madness itself. I screamed in rage- thrusting my fist on the car as the harsh reality sank within me. Why can't I protect them? Why did they have to die? Why? Why?!

"Please wake up!"

The further my rage continued... And there was... Something else there. I calmed the inferno within my soul, and began to have another gaze inside. I began to observe but the sight of the child was unbearable. Once more reminding me of how I was unable to unchain this gruesome and tragic ending. Looking away from the horrendous sight I panted for a moment, collecting what lucid ness I had. Slowly I backed away and observed the car once more- indeed there was something else... Something... It was on the front seat... The drivers side...

"You have to wake up!"

Keeping a slow pace I kept my watchful eye on the car... And there was that... That thing in my mind. What was that? That tall, oddly shaped figure... I saw it once again- but I knew where I was, and I knew that- but...

What is this place? What is... But I shook my head, being careful not to deliberate over the matter. I had to focus on the drivers side- it was rather dark looking in, it was dirty or decayed in some form. And as I came closer my heart began to beat faster, and the tension of the moment began to escalate. I was so nervous without even knowing why- perhaps it was the feeling of suspense in the back of my mind, or the fear of the unknown luring upon me... For whatever reason I felt my heart race as I sweat, panting with a heavy breath as my hand clasped the door... And I moved to open it, fearing what could be on the other side. Wondering... Fearing... Doubting...

"For God's sake!"

I heard the door crack open- its gruesome noise came at such an alarming rate yet I was careful not to flee. It opened, slightly at first... And there...

But... But how?

Standing there I stared in fright- before me was a disturbing outline of blood on the seat. Blood of what appeared to be or has been of a victim. And on the seat was... the victim's clothes. A white shirt, black slacks, a tie with a decorative zig zag pattern in black and white and a pair of shoes...

"No! Please wake up! You have to!"

And the vision... Came back to me once more. And I looked around and saw River Falls. As I looked towards the town I could see that everyone was there. Everyone I knew from my childhood was there as a flood of memories entered my mind.

Yamata-

We always had lunches with each other on Vincent Hill. Her mother was always kind enough to make us a sandwich as we sat in the gentle summer and autumn afternoons. Delighted every time I ate a sandwich she made for me, and we would play childish games like house and hop scotch. It was our own sanctuary as we became best of friends. Then there was one day when she was shy and timid, and asked if when we get older if I would marry her. Of course to this I blushed and said nothing to her irrational question. She giggled to my response- but I always did have a crush on her as a child...

"Someone! Call 911! Please!"

Eric-

I stood there for the first time in his shop with Mom as she was looking for hardware to fix up the house. Eric looked down at me as I felt scared, intimidated by his appearance. He only glared back a me with a sly smile with his arms crossed as I tried to hide myself behind Mom. She checked the aisle looking for the right tool for the job. Yet as time went on I found myself more comfortable with his presence. He would give me advice on what and what not to do- 'Be sure to watch for those critters running loose out there'. Or 'Watch out for your Mom, you hear me?'

He was even considerate enough to show me how to use a gun. Of course he never let me actually shoot one. Or even hold a gun for that matter but he would show one off and talk about how they work...

"Honey- stay back! Get someone to call an ambulance!"

Siri-

She was always an odd woman who seemed very busy. Running to and from the bakery to the police office. As if she did have a twin sister... That was the only conclusion that came to mind as she always ran to and from all over town. I rarely saw her or was able to speak to her. But when I did she was always a kind and considerate individual (even if she didn't seem to be lively at times). She didn't have that much to say except that one time when she was infuriated for some unknown reason. Screaming about how someone stole some of her groceries. it was an important item that belonged to her...

"Come on! You have to wake up!"

Ben moved away a long time ago, around the time of... Yes...

My eighth birthday. I jumped into that pond- that pond that was so majestic as it seemed to shimmer without end. I ran forward to jump in... But something was wrong as I felt myself tripping. As I began to loose momentum I couldn't stop running, and I heard a loud scream from behind- it sounded like Mom but I turned and there was no one to be found... And I didn't see the large stone standing near the pond... And I fell... I fell and I felt my arm shatter as it hit the ground. I began to roll without end as my teeth shattered and my spine broke... Someone was crying... Screaming for help as I lay there... yes it was Mom. She was crying...

"No! Not Matt! No!"

I looked once again in the car as I saw the dead child and the bloody clothes that lay on the seat. I couldn't bare its horrid site or stench as I turned away and shut the door in disgust. And I looked once more towards town- indeed everyone was there. I saw they were all there, waiting for me to come home after being gone for so long, after being lost. They all lay out there in town... dead. They lay there waiting for me to join them at long last as I have been looking for so long. And here I am long last in River Falls. Don't cry Mother... The doctor with those big scary eyes was able to prepare me... Now he's here too, with everyone else.

And we'll be together...

Together...

Also by William Schumpert

Fright Vault
Fright Vault Volume 1
Fright Vault Volume 2
Fright Vault Volume 3
Fright Vault Volume 4
Fright Vault Volume 5
Fright Vault Volume 6
Fright Vault Volume 7
Fright Vault Volume 8
Fright Vault Volume 9
Fright Vault Volume 10

Standalone
The Rhymes of Madness
Grandma's Town
The Lakefront
Once Distant
Sweet Daisy
Capsule X
D.E.Y.E.
Epilogue

Watch for more at https://books2read.com/ap/RDM6kr/William-Schumpert.

About the Author

William Schumpert is an author and illustrator born and raised in Oklahoma; he graduated Southern Nazarene University in 2009 with a Bachelor's Degree in Art and Mass Communication and enjoys writing poetry, horror and short stories.

Read more at https://books2read.com/ap/RDM6kr/William-Schumpert.